THE RAINBOW SUMMER

After a broken romance in America, Lorraine returns to England, to the shelter of her cousin Monica's new home, The Lodge. There, Lorraine's heartache soon takes second place to the problems she encounters. When they decide to turn The Lodge into a drop-in cafe, a young stranger is hired as a temporary gardener/ handyman. Tim, who has a little girl called Angel, is a great help — but Lorraine cannot rest easy until she knows the secret he is trying so hard to hide . . .

Books by Mavis Thomas
in the Linford Romance Library:

HOME IS WHERE THE HEART IS
THE SUNSHINE DAYS
BROKEN MELODY
SECOND CHANCE
SHADOW OVER YESTERDAY

MAVIS THOMAS

THE RAINBOW SUMMER

Complete and Unabridged

LINFORD
Leicester

C206/602
5/7/03

First published in Great Britain in 1993

First Linford Edition
published 2003

British Library CIP Data

Thomas, Mavis
  The rainbow summer.—Large print ed.—
  Linford romance library
  1. Love stories
  2. Large type books
  I. Title
  823.9'14 [F]

  ISBN 0–7089–9459–8

Published by
F. A. Thorpe (Publishing)
Anstey, Leicestershire

Set by Words & Graphics Ltd.
Anstey, Leicestershire
Printed and bound in Great Britain by
T. J. International Ltd., Padstow, Cornwall

This book is printed on acid-free paper

1

It looked as though noone was at the station to meet me. Not the end of the world, of course. It would surely be no great problem to find a taxi, but this was a disquieting end to a long journey. After travelling all the way from New York, USA, to semi-rural Sussex, England, I had hoped at least for a welcoming face.

Perhaps, after all, I should have let Max drive me down from London this morning as he so much wanted to do. At the time, it had seemed the most sensible thing to insist on a quick goodbye. I couldn't help not caring for him as he cared for me. It was no use dragging out the misery by pretending I ever could . . .

'Are you Miss Harrison?' a voice hailed me, and I turned quickly.

'I am! Lorraine Harrison. I was

expecting my cousin Monica to be here — '

'I know. Sorry, you've got me instead. I'm Imogen Hale — her sister-in-law, you know? I expect she told you I'm here a few weeks helping with the café. Oh, sorry I'm late, I stopped off to make a phone call — it's hopeless ringing Wayne from the house, everyone hovers round with ears flapping!'

'Nice of you to come, Imogen. Sorry I didn't recognise you,' I apologised.

'No reason why you should, I was only a kid when I was Monica's bridesmaid — I wouldn't have known you either,' she said airily. 'We had a few hungry hikers in the café this lunchtime, and Monny thought I couldn't cope — so she sent me here to meet you and she's up to her eyes in the ham rolls and pizzas!'

She grabbed one of my cases and said, 'Come on, the car's just outside — and come to think of it, I left the baby in it. Let's cart this stuff along.'

Imogen would be about nineteen

now, I supposed, counting back to the day when Monica married Graham Hale — and the effervescent, schoolgirl bridesmaid who almost upset their wedding cake. She hadn't changed that much, slim, chestnut-haired and assured. Monica had mentioned on the telephone that Imogen was spending most of her summer vacation working at the café/guesthouse which was my cousin's brave new venture. If indeed 'working' was the right word. I recalled Monica's edged comments.

With belated concern I asked, 'Is Monica all right? How is she?'

Mother of three young children, Monica had been widowed a little more than two years ago. I deeply admired her courage and fortitude. It was just unfortunate that she and I had always been more like sparring partners than bosom buddies whenever our paths crossed — maybe, because we were about as alike as the proverbial chalk and cheese. I always had, so people said, a bright and bubbly personality

— and Monica had never bubbled in her life.

'Um,' Imogen said vaguely, beginning to toss my goods and chattels wholesale into a tatty, roomy old Ford, already laden with boxes of provisions and not least a sticky-faced, half-asleep toddler, strapped into a travel-seat. 'She gets tired. She's terribly wrapped up in the business — and worried because it isn't doing well. And the children can be a real pain — I'm not sure which is worse, minding them or washing up. I can tell you, being here is no picnic.'

'Never mind, I'll be another shoulder to the wheel!' I consoled her.

'But you're on holiday!' she protested.

She went on grumbling disjointedly about the guesthouse and the rustic dullness of its environs, pausing merely to unwrap a lollipop and thrust it into the child's hand, as his big, blue eyes opened and his lower lip began to tremble.

'Get his mouth filled up before he opens it to start screaming, that usually works,' she said succinctly. 'Can you squeeze in somewhere?'

I managed, with difficulty. Over my shoulder I tried a friendly, 'Hello there, Barney!' and 'Aren't you a big boy, Barney?' with no other result than a great deal of sucking and slurping dangerously close to the back of my neck. Meanwhile, Imogen was steering the car with rather alarming speed across town.

Once out on the open road, she began asking about my work, the travel and hotels and 'famous people' with whom I mixed. I rambled on about eccentric conductors, temperamental divas and prima ballerinas. Less easy to satisfy was her curiosity about Damien Clyde. I had vowed to myself not to think about him — nor the roses he gave me on my last birthday, the tête-a-tête late dinners, the drives and rushes for planes and long, quiet hours working, nor his voice, his smile, the dreams I had dreamed . . .

'We're here!' Imogen finally announced.

She waved a proprietary hand at a notice adorning a tree trunk. THE LODGE — TEAS, ACCOM, PARKING, DRIVE IN 200 YARDS. 'We're Deep Well Lodge, actually. I told Mon to forget that, it sounds too grim.'

'Do you have a deep well?' I asked.

'There's supposed to be one somewhere. We also have creepy cellars and leaky attics, and a lot of tumbledown stables and storehouses. Probably a few ghosts of long-dead monks from up the hill, I shouldn't wonder.'

Reserving judgement on all that, I did appreciate her grievance about the location. We were bumping along a rutted lane that really looked like a last outpost of civilisation.

Finally, the long, crumbling wall gave way to a wide gateway, flanked by twin pot-bellied stone birds crouched on pillars.

'Good grief. What do you call those?' I exclaimed.

'I call them hawks. Monny calls them eagles.'

'Vultures,' I decided. 'Very definitely vultures.'

She giggled explosively, turning into the entrance and up a wide, gravelled drive. My first impression of the house perhaps owed less to Imogen's comments than to those guardian birds: a vista of high grey roofs and pointed gables, whitened walls, higgledy-piggledy windows and one tall arched one probably lighting the staircase. It stood against a backcloth of trees in a spread of grounds that had once been landscaped with walks and raised beds and statues, but had reverted partly to their natural state.

'Hideous, eh?' Imogen asked candidly.

'I wouldn't say that. It's certainly big. It has — character.'

'Huh! Give me something modern every time. This was the only place cheap enough for Monny to buy,' she commented with even more embarrassing candour. 'The former owner bought it as a derelict, had it partly converted and furnished and then was taken ill before ever opening the place. No goodwill with the business, just 'potential.' Potential for too much hard work if you ask me. All right, Barney,' she hushed some insistent whimperings. 'You'll be back with Mummy in just a minute!'

Imogen crunched the car to a standstill on weed-encroached gravel.

Barney was just becoming seriously vocal, and she looked none too keen to handle his moist presence. I stooped inexpertly to unfasten him from his seat, and he thrashed protesting chubby legs.

'I'll do it!' a sharp voice said behind me.

Capable hands scooped the child up. I looked round at my cousin with an over-bright greeting, 'Monica! — Lovely to see you, how are you?'

However she was, she had aged since our last meeting. My senior by three years, so still just short of thirty, I saw that loss and grief and struggle had laid their mark upon her.

'I'm fine, thank you.' The piercing, pale grey eyes examined me. 'How are you? You look very stylish as usual. Much the same.'

'Not quite, can't you see the extra inch all round — too much pasta when we were in Italy last winter researching for the latest book!'

She raised one eyebrow in that aggravating way she had. I pressed on quickly. 'Monny, I hope you didn't mind me ringing out of the blue and inviting myself here. You see, I arranged very suddenly to come back to England, and then realised I had nowhere to go . . . now Dad's virtually settled in Norway with his oil-rigs there's no 'home' to come back to — '

Monica was silent as she mopped up Barney's sticky face.

'It's all right. I'm pleased to have you here, Lorraine. I mean that,' she said.

I believed she did. Poor Monica. I felt guiltily I should have kept more closely in touch with her, done far more to help her long before now.

'Imogen will show you your room,' she said abruptly. 'Then come down for some tea.'

Smiling my thanks, I was already glad I had come. It was nice to be welcomed and needed somewhere — now that I knew Damien Clyde didn't need me.

Imogen flourished a proprietary hand. 'The hall! Quite imposing with that church window effect. Of course, the decor is foul. Sort of stale porridge with a touch of curdled sludge, would you say — but whoever went to town with all that shell-pink paint made it worse instead of better!'

About to ask, 'Where are the children?' I found my question answered, unspoken. A door opened and voices clamoured, 'The video's stuck! — Aunt Gen, please will you fix it?

'We're watching the Toxic Crusaders — oh!'

Two pairs of Monica's pale, grey eyes

regarded me with curiosity. Imogen explained carelessly. 'This is your Auntie Lorraine. Mummy's cousin. They were brought up together as little girls, years and years ago.'

'Not so many of the years and years, if you don't mind. How are you doing, Greg? And Sarah, my goodness you've both grown big! I'm just exploring your huge new home,' I encouraged. 'Isn't it exciting living here?'

Four-year-old flame-haired Sarah, with the delicate face of a china doll, stared silently. Six-year-old Greg, snub-nosed, built like a miniature weight-lifter, his glaring red hair matched by an archipeligo of freckles, shrugged.

'No it's not. Birds singing. People eating. Grandpa snoring. That's all.'

'Grandpa Hale,' Imogen amplified. 'Supposed to be here on his hols. But what do you bet he's really here for good?'

'Imogen, even without any B and B's you've got a full house here!' I gasped.

'Don't tell me.' She shook her head

gloomily. 'I keep telling Mon she's got to install a dishwasher. But she thinks she's already got one. Me!'

Imogen promised to fix the video later, and continued her grand tour. Upstairs along a rambling landing, she pointed out doors and finally flung one open.

'Yours. The best guest room.'

'I told Monica any old corner would do! When you get a booking, I'll shift.'

'Don't worry, we've more rooms, plus attics. People don't stay here. Can't blame them,' she said candidly.

'But I'm sure that could be changed! The right sort of publicity — '

Obviously not interested, she perched on the edge of the bed while I looked around. It was a pleasant enough room, newly painted in apple green, the window overlooking the garden. I started opening the suitcase I had brought up.

'Tell me some more about your work,' she pressed wistfully.

She wasn't to know how painful it

was to look back. I smiled brightly.

'Oh, like I said in the car — Mr Clyde does a lot of research, he interviews people. That means typing tapes and notes, arranging tickets and itineraries — and you always have social events or performances to attend just when you feel like an early night!'

'But you enjoy every minute. Don't you?'

'Some of it has been good. Yes, some of it.'

'You don't sound too sure.' Her face lighted at a new thought. 'Does he make too many passes at you?'

'Damien? My dear, he wouldn't demean himself. Apart from being too busy — and too bad-tempered, he must have come from a long line of rattlesnakes!' I saw that face in the mirror laughing its ready laugh that hid so much. 'Imogen, why don't you lend Monny a hand while I freshen up? I'll be down directly.'

In under ten minutes I was seated at one of those white tables on the grass, with tea and sandwiches. Monica was bustling to and fro, with Barney ensconsed in a playpen by the house, and a trio of students, evidently fresh from the Ruins, debating her scribbled menu. She looked, I thought now, quite desperately tired.

I couldn't sit there and watch. Gulping down the last of the tea, I found my way back inside, through one of the 'Private' doors into a very large, bare, buff-coloured kitchen that had once housed an open range.

I seized an apron from a hook. A passing Monica, offloading more crockery, snapped in her severe way, 'You're on holiday. And you'll ruin your nail-varnish!'

'That's not important. I hate doing nothing. I'm not used to it.'

'Well, if you must,' she said gruffly. 'I need a round of ham salad on brown, easy on the mayonaisse, a lime milkshake, and a toasted cheese sandwich. Think you can cope with that?'

'Certainly. Just show me where

everything is,' I offered rashly.

When Imogen warned me life at The Lodge was 'no picnic' she wasn't far wrong. I found myself snatched up in an unfamiliar whirl of scorching toast and dismembering salad and almost wrecking the milkshake mixer.

In the midst of it all, the telephone rang in the hall. I dived to answer it. It could be Damien, calling to tell me I was missed, I must get myself on the next plane back to him . . .

'The Lodge Café-Guesthouse, may I help you?' I chirped.

A familiar voice indeed — but not Damien's — 'Lorraine? I just wanted to know you'd arrived safely.'

'Yes, I arrived, Max.' I took a deep breath. 'Nice of you to ring — but there's simply no need to worry about me.'

I could hear traffic bowling past. He was in a callbox somewhere. I imagined the blue-eyed, sensitive face filled with its anxiety for me.

'You haven't reached your mother's

yet?' I asked unnecessarily.

'Not quite. I'll be there soon.'

'I hope you find her well,' I said politely, trying not to sound impatient. 'And thanks again for calling, but I really am very busy just at the moment . . . '

It wouldn't be the last call. I wished there was more I could say to him.

Turning away from the phone, I recalled Imogen's hint about the lack of privacy. She, herself, was assiduously rubbing smears off the banisters. Monica was in the kitchen doorway. More than likely, Grandpa had an ear to his keyhole.

'Max? Sounds interesting!' Imogen hinted.

'You mind your own business, miss!' Monica admonished her sharply.

'It's all right. He's Damien Clyde's brother, an architect. We've met up a few times and we came back together yesterday. And he's just a friend.' I said.

Suddenly, feeling the need for some fresh air, I walked straight through the kitchen and out to the garden.

Outside, the sun was blinding. The trickle of customers had petered out. Resignedly, I started piling used crockery on to a tray.

Then I glanced up, aware of being watched. A man, carrying a drowsy child in his arms, had ventured past the vultures by the gateway, but seemed uncertain whether to come in any farther.

'Excuse me!' I called across brightly. 'Do come in! We're not closed, just having a little lull. Can I get you something?'

For a moment he took no notice of me at all, still surveying the surroundings through dark concealing sunglasses. There was, I thought, something striking about him, but I couldn't decide what it was.

'What will it be? Tea? Cold drinks? How about ice-cream?' I suggested.

'Oh. Sorry!' His attention turned to me. 'Just a quick cuppa . . . an orange drink for the Sleeping Beauty here. Thanks very much!'

I indicated a table in the shade, and bent sympathetically to the little girl who was just opening large, unexpectedly dark eyes.

'Hello, poppet! You look worn out. Has Daddy been walking you too far?'

'Miles and miles. And miles.' They were quick and sharp and full of intelligence, those eyes. 'I'm not called Poppet, I'm Angelique. Angel for short.'

'Angel. Just the right name for you,' I approved.

Back inside, I called to Monica that I could manage, and put together a tray, adding a plate of her home-made sultana scones.

'I know you didn't order them. On the house!' I told Angelique's father — a good way to boost Monica's faltering profits. I was turning away when he called me back.

'Hang on! How long has this place been open?'

'Not long. Not very long at all.' I was quite pleased to 'hang on'. 'We do bed and breakfast, too. Very reasonable. All

18

genuine home cooking!'

'Are you in charge here?'

'No! I'm just helping out. Actually, this is my first day. My cousin, Mrs Hale, is the owner.'

'I see. Does Mrs Hale need any temporary help for the summer? Gardening, cleaning, decorating? I'll do just about anything.'

'I'm not at all sure Monica wants anyone. The business hasn't really got going yet, you see.'

'I've had café experience. All sorts of experience. I could be useful.'

I surveyed him doubtfully. 'It's fairly tough going. I'm not sure if — '

'All right, I wouldn't qualify for Mr Mega-Muscles, Nineteen-Ninety. I've been ill recently, that's all.'

Looking more closely into his face, I thought it must have been some grave sickness that imprinted those lines and shadows.

'Not pretty, but not quite Phantom of the Opera standard,' he suggested. 'I wouldn't scare off the customers. And

I'm kind to children and animals.'

'Oh, I do beg your pardon.' I felt my face burning. 'Look, you sit here and enjoy your tea. I'll do my best for you. I'll ask my cousin right now!'

In fact, there was no need to do that. She must have been observing, with disapproval, my 'chatting up' her clientele.

'What will you ask me? Is there a problem here?' she asked sharply.

The stranger was obviously quite capable of doing his own asking. I mouthed at him, 'Good luck!' and made myself scarce.

Later in the afternoon, I took time out to escape to my room and hang up some clothes. Downstairs, I realised a major sweeping and mopping and rubbing down of tables and chairs was in process. Monica had just hung a 'Closed' sign on the gate. I could hear Greg bombing up and down the drive on a bike, while Barney's wailing drifted from his playpen. Sarah was dreamily picking wild flowers on the wide spread of grass long overdue for mowing. I hurried down to lend a hand.

'All jolly fun, didn't I warn you?' Imogen asked me. She was sporting mauve rubber gloves and a plastic apron lettered 'Kitchen Slave'. Now don't you wish you'd stayed with your fabulous Mr Clyde?'

'Maybe. Maybe not,' I evaded.

Somehow, Monica had managed to put together a family meal. She was dishing it up in the kitchen.

'You don't mind eating here do you, Lorraine, there's no point in carting everything into the other room just for ourselves — '

'Of course I don't mind,' I said, really wondering that anyone could look any more food in the face at all.

She gathered in the children, and we all sat round the long table at one end of the kitchen, joined creakily by Grandpa Hale — revealed now as a leather-faced, old gentleman of once military bearing, with a clipped moustache and sparse white hair. It was still very warm, and the room seemed airless. I would far rather have wandered away by myself to seek a breeze under the trees.

'Grandpa, did you ever meet my cousin? Lorraine, Graham's grandfather,' she introduced us.

'How do you do, young lady! So you're here to help Monica, are you?' he said gruffly.

'Grandpa,' Monica interrupted, 'I've told you, she's on holiday.'

He grunted. 'She can still do a hand's turn for you, I dare say! You're wearing yourself into the ground. It's time you had some proper help about the place.'

I smiled lamely, but was occupied for the next few minutes by Barney, cheerfully catapulting spoonfuls of food from his high-chair, scoring a direct hit on the shirt I had just changed into. I reached for a cloth to wipe away the mess.

It was a surprise to hear Monica inform everyone, 'Well, there'll soon be some more help around. I'm having the garden cleared up, the decorating finished, et cetera — just a temporary worker, he's called Tim East and he'll be living-in for a few weeks with his little daughter. As from tomorrow!'

It seemed Angelique's father was willing to do any sort of work required for any sort of pay offered, so long as he and the child — especially the child — had a roof over their heads while he 'got sorted out'. He had been seriously injured in a road accident, entailing a lengthy stay in hospital, and had just rescued 'Angel' from a long-term minder with whom she had been very unhappy.

'So why hasn't he got a home to go to? Why is he toting the kid round the countryside with no visible means of support?' Imogen wanted to know. 'And where's the child's mother all this time?'

'I didn't hold an inquisition! It's a short-term arrangement, a simple case of supply and demand,' Monica squashed her curiosity smartly. 'No, Greg, you sit there till you've eaten all those vegetables! The same goes for you, Sarah! No more television today. You've both got square eyeballs already . . . !'

Somehow, I sat through the meal. Conversation dragged, except for Imogen telling me about her boy-friend, Wayne, unfortunately domiciled in London while she was buried here in deepest Sussex. I made duly interested noises.

It was later in the evening before finally I could talk to Monica in private.

If I had it in mind we could relax now for a quiet hour, disillusionment came quickly. In the kitchen yet again, the oven was heating and businesslike packets of flour and mixing bowls were laid out.

'Well, I've heard of workaholics. This is just ridiculous,' I exclaimed.

'If you offer genuine, home-baked cakes, you can't just stock up from a supermarket. Sit down and watch, if you want.'

'Certainly not. I'll help!' I seized

Imogen's 'Kitchen Slave' apron — realising the slogan wasn't really so far from the truth.

We began work, and we worked hard.

'Imogen said the business isn't going too well,' I ventured. 'But — '

'Imogen has a big mouth! Obviously the place needs some building up.'

'That's what I was going to say. I think you've coped wonderfully. Facing up to the big decision to move here — and I'm sure it's for the best.'

'I don't know. It was a risk coming here — there's poor old Grandad's money in it as well as all mine, he insisted on it — he's been very good to me. As for the kids, they need their father.'

'If you want to talk about Graham, Monny — please, I'm here to listen. I'm afraid I didn't know him very well.'

'It's no use looking back,' Monica said sharply. 'Tell me about you!'

'About me? Oh, we've been tremendously busy! Researching the opera book, and then there was the new ballet season — and the Zeon Lubitz Tour . . . '

Lamely, I trailed off. Her shrewd direct eyes didn't miss much.

'I didn't ask about the Zeon Whatsit Tour, I asked about you.'

I sat down suddenly by the table, scattering more flour.

'Monica, I'm in all sorts of trouble. I really came here to think things over. I — I just don't know what I'm going to do . . . '

It wasn't my intention to tell her the truth, she who had problems enough. Yet now there seemed no way of holding back the great tide of emotion that obsessed me by day and haunted my sleep by night.

'You see, I'm not here on holiday. I'm not going back, not ever!'

'Are you saying you've given up your job? I don't believe it, Lorraine!'

Well might she stare, knowing that exciting, absorbing, all demanding job had been my whole world.

'I gave Damien Clyde my notice.

He told me to go straight away, he could replace me any time . . . charming, after all this while! But I had to leave, because — because I love him.'

'Of course. I've guessed that a long time,' Monica said calmly enough.

'Well, let's hope I'm not as obvious to him, too! You see, I really thought it would work out. I thought he cared for me a little. He always wanted me there — not just when I had to make notes and arrangements. We had these cosy dinners when we talked and talked . . . and on my birthday he gave me this whole armful of crimson roses, you've never seen such roses!'

For a moment my voice choked. I steadied it furiously.

'So last month,' I ploughed on, 'we went on this South American trip. There was an American violinist touring — she's just won the Jan Hollof Award — and we kept meeting up with her. Cecilia Brand is twenty-something, she has long, blonde hair, even longer legs, eyes like gentians . . . There was a party where Damien danced with her all night. Another time they went off on someone's boat. Finally, we all got back to New York. I brought back a gorgeous tan — Damien brought back a fiancée. Maybe not quite officially — but the last thing I knew they were looking around for a ring . . . '

'I see,' Monica said succinctly. 'That's tough.'

'The maddening thing is, I tried so hard not to care for him! I kept telling myself I stayed on because of the interesting work. All the time I wouldn't believe I just wanted to be with him, heaven help me! But when this Cecilia Brand arrived, I knew for sure, I had to face it. And I couldn't just stay and watch them get married, how could I?'

'Not very easily. Not feeling as you obviously do.'

'So I told him I wanted a change, I

had to help out a relative who'd started up a country hotel. I used you as a lame excuse, sorry about that — '

'No need. I'd say you did absolutely right to walk out!'

'You think so? Perhaps it was running away.'

'No! You're giving him a chance he doesn't deserve to come to his senses. Ten to one you'll hear from him soon. That's the moment when you'll really have to make the biggest decision — whether you still want him. Speaking purely as an observer, I'd say you're better off without him!'

'No,' I whispered. 'I've never felt the same about anyone as I've felt about Damien. It . . . it's special. Very special.'

'Maybe. You know your own business best.'

'But — that isn't quite all the problem,' I had to admit.

'You mean there's more?' she exclaimed.

'Damien has a younger brother. The one who rang me earlier today. Maxwell isn't much like him — 'just a run of the mill architect who doesn't know his Brahms from his Beethoven' Max always says . . . His wife died a while back, I don't know the details. Lately, I've got the feeling he's following me around. He kept on visiting in New York, he travelled back with me yesterday to stay with his mother — he might be taking up a post in London, and I wonder if it's just an excuse to stay in reach . . . He's such a nice guy, I hate to hurt him! But I can't pretend, can I? Though he's probably worth two of Damien.'

'Dear me,' Monica said inadequately. 'I see the problem. Yes, I suppose if you play the field, life does get this complicated!'

It was a typical Monica Hale comment, of course.

'There's something my Graham often said — I reckon we both need to hang on to it. 'Storms can end in rainbows, and rainbows can end in pots of gold.' Sounds corny, but you never know.'

Left alone in the big kitchen with its

pleasant aroma of baking, I just went on sitting there. Outside, that belated dusk had finally settled down over the trees. A nightingale was pouring forth a deluge of song, very beautiful, very sad.

Maybe that rainbow was out there somewhere, but it was going to take some finding.

2

By now I should have been used to sleeping in new locations, under unfamiliar roofs, but it didn't always work that way. Tonight's problem wasn't so much the difference between the air-conditioned cocoon of a New York hotel and this old house among its towering trees so full of vague rustlings and the unnerving sound of an owl, as my troubled mind telling me I had made my final break, and yesterday's world was gone for ever. It was a scary idea.

Apart from all that, Deep Well Lodge possessed its own kind of disturbing night life. Ancient floorboards creaked and plumbing gurgled. A child was continually coughing and crying out — that would be little Sarah. Greg was prowling round for a drink, hissed at sharply on the landing to go to bed and stay there.

At one stage I opened my door to see Monica, her long, bright hair loose around her shoulders, hurrying past with cough syrup and drinks on a tray. She insisted there was no way I could help.

I heard eventually a frenzied 'dawn chorus' of chirps and cheeps from neighbouring branches. The next time I opened bleary eyes, it was past nine o'clock. In businesslike jeans and check shirt, I hastened down to find my cousin.

'Morning,' I said brightly. 'Sorry I'm so late, I meant to bring you tea in bed!'

'No need. I'm always up early — Barney wakes around five,' Monica replied.

'Well, at least it's Sunday. We can have a long peaceful day in the sun — ' I started to say, and then had a sudden thought. 'Or is the café open on Sundays?'

'It is. It has to be. I can't afford not to open.'

Stupidly, it hadn't struck me. Of

course, Sundays with Damien were often occupied with typing notes, maybe taking in some celebrity recital. This was something different. I thought of all the cleaning up we did last night. It seemed a sin to dirty anything ever again.

'Someone rang you,' Monica added, dumping toast and coffee on the kitchen table. 'He said he'd ring back.'

I felt my heart starting to race. 'Did he — give a name?'

'He just said he'd ring when he and his mother returned from church.'

'Max,' I said tonelessly.

Through the wide open window I could see the children in the garden, Barney busily trying to decapitate a teddy in his play-pen.

Already it looked as though yesterday's heat would be surpassed today. The sun was doing its best to exterminate Monica's tubs of drooping flowers by the drive. I went for a speculative wander round the grounds, the fenced-off area marked 'Private' which I hadn't managed to explore yesterday.

A sudden sound behind me, when I imagined myself alone with birds and insects and ghosts, was a real shock. It was hard to know who gave the bigger start, myself or the intruder.

'Sorry, but you're trespassing! This isn't open to the public — ' I started to say severely, and then stopped short. I wasn't addressing a complete stranger. 'Oh, it's you. I'm not too sure of your name — '

'East. Tim East.'

'Lorraine Harrison. Welcome! What are you doing out here!'

'Being nosey,' he answered with that immediacy of response I had noticed before. 'We just arrived — I left Angel with our luggage. But there's a panic on inside, they can't deal with us yet, so I came to see what sort of gardening and repairing I've let myself in for ... A right load of graft, wouldn't you say?'

'I would say. But I hope you're not having second thoughts about the job.'

'Some. I didn't plan to stay long. And this lot would make a professional throw a wobbly.' He smiled unexpectedly ruefully.

'A large sized wobbly.' I smiled back. 'But please give it a go. My cousin has had a rough time, and this place *must* succeed. If it flops, I don't know what the effect on her would be. What was that about a crisis indoors?'

'A kid screaming. People shouting and rushing about.'

'That sounds like the norm for this place, but I'd better find out. Coming?' I invited. 'And you will stick with the job? I'll deem it a personal favour.'

'Put like that, how can I possibly refuse?' he answered my sincere appeal.

I forgot all about Tim the next moment, as we hurried round to the house where Angelique was perched on two large shabby suitcases. Imogen, tearing down from the bathroom with towels and cotton-wool, called to me dramatically, 'Barney fell over in the kitchen! There's blood simply everywhere!'

It was a picturesque exaggeration, but the reality was serious enough. Amid piles of abandoned sandwiches, and something burning horribly on the stove, the little boy had obviously tripped over a yellow duck on wheels and hit his head either on the tiles or a table leg. His face was streaming with blood and tears as Monica, squatting on the floor, cradled him in her lap.

'I thought you were watching him — '

Monica snapped at Imogen. 'Oh, of course, I always get blamed for everything! — '

Nerves were taut with anxiety — and in Monica's case also with long-standing strain. It wasn't like her to waste time on acrimonious words when actions were urgently needed.

'Look,' I suggested, 'calm down, everyone! Where's the nearest doctor? Can I try to phone for you?'

'Excuse me barging in — ' another voice cut me short, ' — but just cover him up well — because of shock, right?

Wrap his head in a clean towel. I saw there's a hospital in the town, run him straight along to Casualty!' Tim East, kneeling now beside Monica, spoke as one who knew. 'This may need a couple of stitches but it's fairly superficial. Shouldn't be any problem.'

'Oh. Well. You're probably right,' Monica agreed, surprised into meekness.

'I'll drive you, Monny,' Imogen volunteered at once. 'I'll get the car started!'

In some strange way, order resolved from chaos. Of course I would keep an eye on Greg and Sarah, I promised — and make Grandpa a soothing cup of tea — and if necessary finish off the half-made sandwiches.

Monica shook her head at the last idea.

'Don't bother. Just keep the CLOSED sign on the gate. Today's going to be another write-off. One of many.'

She climbed into the back of the big car, with Barney, now quiet and subdued, on her lap. I squinted after them down the sunny driveway. From somewhere in the town the distant sound of Sunday morning church-bells wavered.

★   ★   ★

In my life with Damien Clyde over the past months and years, organisation had been very much the name of the game — mingled with a good measure of tact and diplomacy. It looked to me as though all three would be necessities today.

'Yes, Greg, I suppose you can ride your bike in the garden,' I told him. 'But carefully, please, we don't want any more disasters!'

Looking round I met full and square the startlingly bright 'streetwise' eyes of Angelique. It was the same quality her father had.

'Now why don't you and Sarah,' I urged her, 'pick me some pretty posies of flowers for the café tables? Wild ones will do as long as they're nice and bright, and nice leaves. We're going to open up today in style!'

'Mummy said the café's closed. She'll be ever so cross,' Sarah quavered.

'Oh, I'm sure she won't. She was just upset and in a big hurry.' I turned hopefully to Tim East. 'I just thought, why waste a sunny Sunday, with starving day-trippers marching all over the Abbey Ruins? Maybe not a full menu, but wouldn't drinks and snacks be better than nothing?'

'Sounds like common-sense. I was going to suggest the same thing.'

'You were? Good thinking! Shall we get started?'

Before eleven, the depressing CLOSED sign was changed to an inviting OPEN. Every table was cheery with an erratic flower arrangement. The children were on watch for customers outside or — a remote chance — the phone ringing inside with a prospective bed-and-breakfast booking. Water was boiling, an array of sandwiches and snacks awaited mouths to eat them. Even Grandpa, though insisting no good would come of it, began clipping a shaggy hedge by the gate.

I couldn't quite believe it when an overheated trio of hikers trailed in, and then a car nosed doubtfully up the drive — and especially a bevy of youngsters in shorts and T-shirts bounced in wanting ice-cold Cokes and late fry-up breakfasts.

'I'll see what we can do! — Where did you all spring from?' I asked.

'The Camping Park over the back,' a tall teenager informed me.

'Well, I'm glad to hear it! Listen,' I inveigled her, 'free Cokes all round if you'll spread the word about us. I'll give you a poster to hang up somewhere!'

I panted out the story quite excitedly to my colleague in the kitchen, and was highly relieved to find him quite ready to do the cooking. While he dropped bacon and eggs and mushrooms into a pan, I scorched toast and over-simmered beans. When we ferried the platefuls outside, the couple from the car wanted more sandwiches. Two newcomers were just arriving.

'And a chunk of that fruit pie! — and another coffee, Timothy!' I called in at the doorway. I giggled. 'It sounds as though we've got a chef — they'll be expecting real Cordon Bleu cuisine!'

'They're getting real Cordon Bleu, aren't they?' Tim answered.

'From you. Certainly not from me.

The time was passing, and we had no word from Monica. Really I had expected her back by now, or at least a telephone call. A vague alarm bell was starting to clang in my mind and wouldn't be silenced. The café trade was lagging. Greg stumped into the kitchen, followed by his silent little sister, to announce that they were both mega-mega-starving — which no doubt they were.

Promising a prompt meal, I said, 'Aren't you going to fetch Angelique to join us? — you've left her all on her own.'

'Angelique.' Greg pulled a face of

derision. 'Fancy being called that!'

I realised that in fact the dark-eyed child was standing in the doorway. She was clearly well able to stand up for herself.

'It's French, what's wrong with it? It's my grandmother's name. She lived in Paris, she did. She was a dancer. On the stage in real theatres, I've got pictures of her! And I can dance, too. Shall I show you?'

'I'm sure you can, Angel,' I mollified her hastily, 'but not just now — and definitely not in this kitchen! It's far too dangerous in here.'

When the phone did ring, I had taken out a tray to a lone, new customer. An urgent voice shouted to me, 'Lorraine, it's Imogen! Hurry up!'

I ran headlong but I was too late, Imogen had been ringing from a pay-phone.

'Tim, couldn't you have called me sooner?' I exploded.

'Sorry. She said she'd get more change and call back. I took the message anyway. Do you want the good news or the bad news?'

So those alarm bells hadn't been ringing for nothing. I waited mutely.

'The kid's fine, he can come home. But Mrs Hale fell down the stairs.'

'Monica fell . . . ?' I repeated dully. 'I don't believe this. I just don't.'

'Gospel truth. She hurt her leg mainly. Nothing too desperate, but she's staying there tonight for sure — maybe longer.'

I looked at the man quietly waiting for me to assimilate his news. I didn't know him either. It was just odd that, after half a day, I felt as though I did.

'You told me this morning,' I said abruptly, 'you didn't intend staying long. It might get tough here now, but please, don't walk out on me!'

'Didn't I give you my word I'd stay a while?'

I gave him a rather shaky smile of gratitude . . .

If anyone had suggested yesterday I could spend a whole day with hardly a thought of Damien, or his blonde-haired Cecilia Brand — or even Maxwell Clyde trailing along somewhere in the rear — I would have called it a sheer impossibility.

Yet it was happening. And it went on happening.

Later, Imogen called back. She sounded almost tearful, quite unlike the assured individual who met me the day before at the station. She told me Monica was worried sick, furious with herself for doing such a stupid thing and causing so much trouble. I tried to find words of comfort, offering to get a taxi straight to the hospital.

'No, Monny wants you to stay with the children.'

'But I can see her tonight, can't I? When you're back home?'

'I don't know, she doesn't want anyone. I — I've never seen her like this . . . '

'Imogen, don't worry too much. She's had two bad shocks today,' I said, 'and she's been overworking tremendously as well, hasn't she?'

'I know. She's been so good to me, and — all I did was call her a slave driver and try to dodge all the work.'

'Come on. You've helped her a lot. She told me so! I think she was due for some sort of breakdown — but we'll nurse her back to a far better state of health than before this happened, I promise you!'

I believed I had made an impression. She would be home soon with Barney, she said. Meantime, someone had to break the news to the rest of the family.

Old Mr Hale obviously was very shaken. He thought the world of Monica, her peppery nature notwithstanding. It would be all too easy to dismiss him as a nuisance best left to vegetate under a plaid blanket, but his years and his frailties weren't his fault.

'I'm sure it sounds much worse than it is, Grandpa! And I know we can keep things going here for her between us. How about another cup of tea?'

'She didn't hit her head, did she?' Angelique piped up unexpectedly.

'I don't think so. Why do you ask?' I turned to her curiously.

'Oh. It's just — people who hit their heads in accidents, they get very ill . . . and they're sort of different afterwards, sort of really strange . . . '

She stopped abruptly as her father came into the room. I was reminded anew of the scarring on his forehead, and maybe those dark-lensed glasses he hadn't discarded since he arrived . . . However this was no time to wonder about any mysteries surrounding the 'hired help'. It was enough to have him there.

For it was he who coped with all the clearing up, when we hoisted the CLOSED notice — with Angel trailing him like a small lively shadow helping to fetch and carry, and even Greg consenting to wipe and stack chairs and collect menus. I found myself tied down with Sarah, whose fright and shock had quite overcome her. I rocked her gently my face against the soft flame-coloured hair. I couldn't remember when I last comforted a child like this. Maybe it was far more fulfilling to hold this living, needing warmth than a chilly pile of Damien's books or files of notes . . .

'Phone, Lorraine!' Angel shouted. She had not only mastered my name, but got to the telephone first. 'It's a man called Max. Sounds nice!'

'Thank you, Angel!' I hushed her hastily.

Of course it was Max. If not Imogen, again, who else?

'Hello again,' I greeted him, with an effort to hide the weariness of anticlimax.

'How are you, Lorraine? Sorry I missed you this morning. I just wanted to know how you're settling down, if you're beginning to enjoy your holiday.'

'Holiday,' I reflected wryly. This man meant so well. He was gentle and kind and concerned. He was just totally in the dark, about a lot of things.

At least there was no need to manufacture small-talk, because I had a dramatic story to pour out — the household and business robbed of its kingpin, the family left adrift, weeping children, tomorrow's menus to sort out . . . 'So you see,' I explained, 'I'm up to my eyes. But it's probably doing me more good than a holiday!'

'I'm not so sure. You looked very tired yesterday.'

'That was yesterday. Max, I'm fine! How is your mother?'

'She's very well, I'm glad to say. I told her about you, we hoped you might come and stay with us — this part of Derbyshire is so beautiful. But — '

'But of course, I can't possibly get away. Thank you both anyway.' I breathed a silent sigh. At least I had got out of that one.

'I understand that. But I do have to come back to London — about my new job — so I'll run down and see you instead. As soon as I can. There must be something I can do to help.'

What could one say? What could one do? I thanked him. The future would have to look after itself.

'One more thing.' He hesitated. 'Have you heard from my brother yet?'

'No, I have *not* heard from your brother yet,' I said sharply.

'I rang him today. He has a new secretary — Marsha someone . . . Marsha Dunlop. She can't understand your filing system, I believe — ' It was as well he couldn't see the effect of those words — I knew my face was a furious scarlet. 'Damien thought he might have to contact you about it.'

'Well, bad luck for him. I'm here if he cares to try, I'm not going anywhere!'

'Only don't let him bother you. Will you?'

The voice in my ear was so anxious. I said guiltily, 'Thank you. No, I won't let him bother me. And I do appreciate you ringing, Max.'

There was no time for more, because I heard tyres scrunching the gravel. Imogen was back with the patched-up Barney. She still looked very upset. Soon, she was sitting down, cradling the forlorn little boy, giving all of us a jumbled account of the accident.

'The stupid thing is there was a lift, of course — but you know Monica, she won't ride if she's got two working feet. She just collapsed on the stairs and rolled down. She was in a real panic when she found she had to stay, I ran out to get her a toothbrush and things and she said, 'Don't drag anyone along tonight, I'll be home tomorrow!' — But I'm not a bit sure she will be . . . '

'Of course she won't. A week at the very least,' Grandpa forecast.

'Let's look on the bright side,' I tried to coax, but someone else had even better words of consolation.

'If you're going to fall downstairs, a hospital is the best place to do it.'

'How true, Tim. How very true!' I agreed.

Imogen looked round at him curiously.

'Oh, I've almost let a double room for tonight. I didn't know how much to charge. Mr and Mrs Parker, they're waiting outside.'

'Good grief. How in the world did you manage that?'

He gave one of his expressive shrugs. 'Once they'd made it past the 'Orrible 'Ens on your gateposts, the rest was dead easy.'

Imogen was still staring as I hastened outside with Tim to clinch the deal. The Parkers proved to be a grey, middle-aged couple with a grey, middle-aged car, pleasant and friendly, quite apologetic about troubling us.

The Parkers were, thankfully, easy to please. I found them a room, Tim produced refreshments, and I hastily whipped assorted clutter from the bathroom and the lounge. At least it would be good news for Monica.

How the rest of that strange timeless day flew past, I wasn't sure. Only I knew I needed ten pairs of hands, plus extra feet to relieve the hot aching ones I already owned. Between us, Tim and I finished off the clearing-up, concocted a family meal, reassured Grandpa that someone would take him to see Monica tomorrow. Imogen, still thoroughly shaken, sat holding a now sleeping Barney with Sarah huddled beside her, and that in itself was help enough. Greg was burning up the driveway on his bike, and Angel had rediscovered the piano.

What the visitors made of their quiet country haven I couldn't imagine. They left presently to drive into town, 'to see the river,' they said.

Mrs Parker stopped on her way out. 'You won't let your little boy ride out in the road, will you? Only these quiet roads can be so dangerous. We stopped at the riding stables to see if they do bed-and-breakfast, but they don't — and the lady advised us to take care cruising around, she said there was once a really bad smash on the bend right near here — didn't she, George?'

'Before we came here, but I've heard about that,' Imogen volunteered. 'Quite gruesome. Someone skidded into a tree. A foreign tourist, so we heard.

Must have been speeding like a maniac, though.'

'George always drives carefully,' Mrs Parker said earnestly. 'Don't you, George?'

Once they'd gone, Imogen and I saw to the children. I found a camp bed for Angel, to fit into a corner of her father's room. Then, we went through the process of light suppers and milky drinks, teeth-cleaning, hair-brushing.

Finally, with my head buzzing, I went for a stroll in the cool solitude of the garden. I turned into the overgrown rear regions where high branches were silhouetted against a limpid evening sky.

Seeking the stone bench I had discovered earlier, I was amazed to find it already occupied.

'You again!' I exclaimed. 'Surely you're not still assessing the work-load of this wilderness?'

Tim didn't answer immediately. I realised he was slumped forward on the low seat. As I touched his shoulder the face he lifted to me, caught in the eerie twilight, shone pale and haggard. At long last he had discarded those tinted glasses, disclosing painfully narrowed eyes as dark as his little daughter's.

'What's wrong?' I sat beside him in quick concern. 'Are you ill?'

'I'm all right. No need to fuss.'

'You're not all right!' I insisted. There flashed into my mind Angelique's words earlier today: 'People who hit their heads . . . afterwards they're really strange . . . ' 'You've probably been working too hard today in the heat — and that's my fault, I should have realised! Shouldn't you see a doctor? Or the hospital where you've been having treatment?'

'They know all about it. Look,' he said sharply, 'Lorraine, will you please do me a favour, just leave me alone? I get headaches sometimes, that's all. Just — don't tell Angel, right?'

'Well — ' I demurred, still unwilling to leave him, then Imogen called into the dusk, 'Lorraine, are you out there?

— A call for you!'

It couldn't be Max again. Not again. I rushed inside, and Imogen greeted me, 'Quick, it's New York — a simply gorgeous voice!' she hissed dramatically.

Still, I didn't believe. Not even when that voice came to me across the miles that divided us.

'How are you, Lorraine? I've had some trouble finding your number. You realise you didn't leave it for me when you walked out?'

Yesterday I would have welcomed a chance to tell Damien Clyde exactly what I thought of his treatment of me. Today, it seemed childish and petty to rake up past wrongs — even though the passage of time hadn't turned them to rights. Chiefly, foolishly, it was wonderful, wholly wonderful, to hear him again speak my name. I had missed him. I knew now just how much.

'It's really you . . . Oh, sorry about the number — but I didn't walk out,' I had to insist, 'I gave you fair notice! You told me just to pack up and go!'

'That's as may be. All water under the bridge. So how are you getting on there?' he asked with that occasional gentleness that was devastating.

'I'm very busy! My cousin who's just opened this guest-house is in hospital after an accident, so — I'm practically running the place at present!'

'So you may have leaped out of the frying-pan into the fire. I'm sorry, Lorraine. Max told me how tired you were looking . . . '

'I'm quite enjoying the work here. At least it's different,' I said gruffly.

'Well, don't overdo it. I won't trouble you for long. But there's something I wanted to ask you — '

If I still clung to any delusions about that tantalising 'but', even after Max's prior warning, they were instantly dashed.

'I have a new secretary-assistant. Fairly organised and efficient, but she's having problems with your index cards — your address system whatever it is. She feels it's rather primitive after searching all day for Matthew Solomons . . . '

'She can't have used much common-sense,' I said tartly. 'He's under 'J' for the Jewish Youth Choir. As he's been running it for years, it's not inappropriate.'

'Ah, right, I'll tell Marsha, she'll be intrigued.'

I choked down an answer. I could picture him so clearly, the lift of his proud dark head, the intensely blue eyes that looked down a slightly aquiline nose upon an inferior world. I wasn't going to let him guess how agitated I was crouched here over the table, my hands clammy, my heart racing.

'I hope your cousin isn't seriously ill?' Damien was saying, and I gave some sort of jumbled explanation.

He probably wasn't interested, but he made a good pretence. 'I hope you find her better tomorrow. Let me know how you get on,' he insisted.

'Yes, I'll let you know,' I promised shakily.

'I wish there was some way I could help. Be sure to ring if there's anything I can do,' he said smoothly.

'In any case, I'll probably see you quite soon. I'm coming to London shortly to start a new project . . . '

Whatever else he added, I made no earthly sense of it.

'You all right?' Imogen was asking curiously, after several minutes of hovering.

'Yes, thank you. I'm fine,' I replied.

Just as easily, I could have turned cartwheels all round the house, warbled from the rooftop in wildest exultation.

3

'At least a week,' Imogen bemoaned. 'That's what they said. And it isn't even certain she'll leave the hospital then, it depends how she gets on. And — and I thought she looked really ill this morning . . . '

It seemed old Mrs Hale's dire prophecies were proving all too accurate. Certainly Monica wouldn't be home this Monday, or for several days to come. Her injured leg had proved serious, not just a straightforward fracture but other damage — 'ligaments and things,' Imogen explained vaguely — and none of it would be helped by her very run-down state.

Imogen had brought us this news after calling at the hospital, having just dropped Greg off at school — too spick and span to be true in navy blazer and pristine white shirt. Grudgingly, he had agreed to go, mainly because there might be a practice for the imminent Sports Day. Sarah, after a miserable night and floods of tears, seemed in no state for a crowded busy school day. In any case, the term was nearly over. A few days absence for her was the least of our present worries.

'There's one good thing,' I said, trying to comfort Imogen, 'Monica needs a thorough rest, most of all. Now she's got to have one! We'd never manage to make her rest here, you know what she's like.'

'I know. But I hate seeing her like this. She didn't want to talk to me — except she said 'be firm with Sarah and take her to school tomorrow no matter what!''

'Let tomorrow take care of itself. Today comes first,' I advised.

In fact, for my own part I was sailing through this difficult day surrounded by some sort of private roseate glow — due of course to Damien Clyde's words last night. I found I could take everything as it came. Tim and I between us got the still earnest and apologetic Parkers breakfasted and the café ready to open. Grandpa was staying late in bed after yesterday, and Barney was unusually quiet and manageable. The woeful Sarah, constantly hanging on to my legs, fortunately was taken firmly under the wing of Angelique — maybe a year older and infinitely her senior in worldly wisdom, assurance, not to say downright cheek.

'I'll look after her,' Angel volunteered. 'Barney, too, if you want. At old Mother Briggs' there was five of us kids — and two of them were much worse than him.'

'There, Imogen,' I told her brightly, 'a capable and willing nursery assistant for you. I was thinking, for today, if you and Angel cope with the shopping and the children and so on, Tim and I can do the café — and later we can all start on some improvements I have in mind. We'll see how things work out. In the future we might swap jobs round to give ourselves a break.'

She looked at me, but didn't appear to resent my taking charge, or ask me who in the world I thought I was. It almost seemed to be a relief to her.

'I need to ring Mum and Dad. They'll want to know about Monny — and send her cards and flowers and things. And I promised Wayne I'd ring him — '

'Go ahead. Take your time,' I told her rashly.

Before she glued herself to the telephone, Tim looked in to announce with a showman-type flourish, 'Expect the Parkers back later, they're exploring Tall Hill and staying another night. Oh, and they're recommending their daughter and family for a week's holiday here.'

'Timothy, you'll make yourself a fortune yet,' I prophesised.

Although I was scarcely more efficient today than yesterday, I did my best not to spill, cremate or generally ruin our menu. Anyway, today I could cope with anything, after Damien's magic phone call. Today, I was convinced that unfortunate, overworked Monica would return to a business set firmly on its feet.

'Can I have a lend of the car for an hour? And can you stand in for me here?' I asked Imogen later that day.

She nodded assent on both counts. 'To see Monny? Is Grandpa going?'

'I'll take him this evening. No, this is shopping. Would there be a house-and-garden store in the town?'

'There's Madderns. Behind the High Street, they've got a car park. But — ' She turned to gaze at me, lifting Barney from his car seat. 'We've got curtains, haven't we? And sunshades?'

'Ah. Monica probably got them cheap in a sale because no-one else fancied them. Wait till you see my selections!'

'But — ' she demurred again. 'I don't know whether her cash flow . . . '

'Never mind her cash flow, this will come out of my cash flow. After all,' I reasoned, 'I thought of taking an expensive, exotic holiday, but I'm not doing that — so why shouldn't I buy something instead?'

Clearly she thought I was crazy, but she handed over the keys. At the last moment, seeing Angel wistfully watching me, I asked her, 'Like to come along and help me? OK, just run and tell your dad.'

I wasn't sure why I did that. My short time at The Lodge had already made me a little more comfortable with the children, but I was still struggling — except with this one child who was in some ways curiously unchildlike.

She settled down in the back of the littered car humming happily.

'You're a musical soul, Angel!' I commented.

'D'you mind me singing? Old Mother Briggs said it got on her nerves.'

'Old Mother Briggs sounds even more disgusting than some of her kids. Sing all you like,' I encouraged. 'Now what colour sunshades do you think would look nice on the patio?'

'I think it all looks nice already. I think the garden's brilliant. And the house. I haven't never ever lived in a place like that before,' she confided earnestly. 'I wish we could stay for years and years. But we don't ever stay. Not since Mummy — '

'Your mummy went away?' I prompted.

'She died, didn't she?'

'I guess maybe she did. I'm very, very sorry,' I said sympathetically.

'It's OK. She lives with the angels, Daddy said. That's why I like being called Angel . . . it's sort of like she still lives with me, isn't it?'

'Of course it is,' I whispered. Busy threading through the town traffic, I wished very much I had an arm free to gather her close to me.

We finished our marathon shopping session at Madderns with a hasty stop at their in-store 'Tea Shoppe'.

'Sorry to rush,' I told her, 'but we must go! There's a lot of work to do — and tonight I'm visiting Mrs Hale at the hospital — '

'Can I come?' she asked at once.

'Maybe you can,' I said. I couldn't exactly tell her that it would probably be one of Monica's children I'd be likely to take.

Back at the house, the café was shut but plenty was going on. Greg had fallen off the swing. Barney was simply being Barney. Sarah couldn't find Oscar the Worm, and wailed that Grandpa had hoed him up. The old gentleman, tackling a little light gardening after a day spent mainly resting, stared none too encouragingly at the cornucopia of goods I began unloading.

'Just a little coming-home present for Monica,' I explained.

'It's very kind of you, young lady. But I'm not sure she should put down too many roots here. This place is too much for her!'

I didn't argue, but Imogen's reactions at least were more cheering.

'Super! You've got great taste, Lorraine!' She whisked round replacing some of the plain sunshades with my floral jobs, laying out colourful place-mats on the outside tables, seersucker cloths inside.

'They're delivering a big stone bath tomorrow,' I said. 'A high one on a twisted column — so Barney can't fall in. And they had to order some of the paint, but we've enough to get started. Nice blending earth colours — a soft 'Terra Cotta Haze' instead of that sickly shell-pink — and Warm Beige, and Desert Glow for part of the kitchen and some of those instant stick-on tiles, I just hope they do stick . . . '

Imogen's eyes opened wider and wider. Absorbed in my schemes, the idea of actually applying the paint with mundane brushes hadn't yet sunk in.

Searching for Tim, I found him lying flat on his face in the grass beside Sarah, delicately manipulating a garden trowel and a jar.

'We've found Oscar's long, lost brother, Fred,' he informed me gravely. 'He's having some trouble with his tail.

We're putting him in that big plant trough with the begonias.'

Before he went in to attend to the family meal, I had another job for him. Grouping flowers around one of the refurbished tables, donning an apron and deftly balancing a tray, I requested my portrait by means of an instant camera.

'Please get in as much of the house as you can — but me and the tables for sure.' I struck a smiling pose in the evening sunshine.

'What's this in aid of, then? Advertising?'

'Just to send to someone,' I evaded.

Tonight, I would enclose this photo in a letter to Damien . . . for did he not make me promise to keep in touch, to let him know how The Lodge worked out? Perhaps, more than any words, the portrait would remind him of the hours he had spent with me . . .

Later, I would sit down to put pen to paper. For the moment, I had no chance. Over Tim's 'chef's special' meal

69

I tried to work out my passenger list for visiting Monica. Grandpa, of course. Greg, who promised to wash and be very quiet; not Barney, likely to disrupt the whole ward and not Sarah, who would weep oceans and upset her mother and herself.

'Tim, will you come? It might ease her mind if you explain how we're coping. And you're due for an hour off duty, if anyone is!' I remarked.

Across the room, Angel's dark eyes pleaded. 'All right,' I told her, 'you might not be able to see Mrs Hale, but come for the ride!'

For the second time I drove off towards the town. The air was hot and heavy. There were rainclouds building up beyond Tall Hill. So long as they did their stuff overnight, I thought, so my floral parasols could come out in force tomorrow.

Eventually we reached the Memorial Hospital, partly an older-style brick building, partly a lower and lighter extension. We bought flowers from a stall by the doorway. As we looked for signposts to Abbey Ward, I escorted the children and Tim gave an arm to old Mr Hale, all at once looking frail and shaky.

Monica's was one of two ground floor wards in the modern wing. There was a small vestibule area with chairs, a telephone and a drinks machine. Also, a notice about a strict maximum of two persons per bedside. I asked, 'Shall I go first, Grandpa? Or will you take Greg in, Monica will want to see close family most of all — '

That was the favoured choice. He went off with a suddenly subdued Greg clutching flowers and chocolates.

Angel, fidgetting on a chair, whispered, 'Yuck, I hate hospitals!'

'But they do make people better. You're not going to be a nurse, then?'

'Course I'm not. I'll be a dancer, won't I?' She wriggled reflectively. 'My mummy was a nurse.'

I gave an interested murmur, but she said no more. Tim sat quietly and still.

Grandpa emerged presently, looking no less upset — and Greg, who had hitherto seemed almost callously unaffected by Monica's accident, suddenly burst into tears. His tough and riotous exterior had been breached. He was a little boy who wanted his mother to come home.

I looked doubtfully at Tim, but he nodded towards the ward.

'You go ahead. They'll be all right.' He had steered Grandpa to a chair, and sorted out coins for the drinks machine. He put a hand on Greg's shoulder. 'Don't worry, your mum'll soon be back home bossing us all around. Come on, who's going to work this machine for me?'

'I will,' Greg muttered gruffly. 'Can — can I have some crisps?'

'Why not? Let's get Mr Hale some tea first, right?'

Greg and Grandpa were in good hands. I slipped nervously in to see Monica. Like Angel, I wasn't very good at hospitals.

The ward was pleasantly light, curtained in gentle green, full of flowers. I picked out Monica's bed at once, led unerringly by her flaming, red hair — though it was screwed back harshly into a plait.

I was shocked just to see Monica the 'workaholic' lying prone and lethargic, her leg beneath a cradle. I was shocked, too, by her pallor, the shadows under her eyes. But she roused to flare at me, 'Grandpa says you're opening the café! All sorts of hours and meals! Didn't I tell you *not* to do that?'

'The café's fine, Monny. Everything's under control, I promise. Tell me how you are, if there's anything at all I can bring you . . . '

She turned her head away, muttering that she was perfectly all right, it was all a fuss about nothing. She did say she was glad to see me. I supposed it was true. But clearly she didn't digest any of the cheery news I recited, the camping park, the B & B's who actually opted for a second night, Tim's great help and capability.

She had a string of anxious questions about Barney. She asked why I had upset Greg by bringing him — and why Sarah hadn't been taken to school. Was Imogen gadding off at all hours to see Wayne in London? Was someone insisting Grandpa took his indigestion medicine? And how in the world could anybody pay attention to all that and run the café properly, too?

'How could you ever expect to do it?' I almost retorted. 'Isn't that the real reason you're lying in that bed nagging me right, left and centre?'

Of course, I choked back the words, but I felt it wouldn't be wise to prolong this visit.

'I'll come again soon, when you're not so tired,' I promised.

'All right. Thank you. Lorraine, it was nice of you to come. Look, can you get me some toothpaste? I asked Imogen but she forgot it — '

'She was upset,' I said gently. 'I'll get

some now from the kiosk.'

It was a good excuse to leave. I didn't know what to say to her.

Outside, Grandpa was sipping tea. I took Greg with me to the small shop run by the Hospital Friends, where I bought him some sweets and his mother toothpaste. Just as we got back, the 'Visitors Out' bell began ringing.

Delivering the toothpaste, I found Tim sitting beside Monica, talking to her quietly and seriously. It struck me she even looked a shade brighter. The unquenchable Angel had attached herself to an elderly lady in the next bed, who had received no callers and looked a little overwhelmed by the visitation.

''Bye, I hope you feel lots better, I'll bring you a get well card,' she promised.

Tim was saying much the same. 'I'll see you again, Mrs Hale.'

She mumbled, 'Yes, come again. And I told you — it's Monica . . . '

Back in the car park we sorted ourselves out and loaded ourselves up.

Old Mr Hale kept asking, 'So what did you think of her?'

'Not a lot,' I had to admit. 'I suppose we can't expect — '

'Painkillers,' Tim said. 'She's on a fair dosage — and I've had enough of them to know what they can do to you. The accounts for the general lethargy. Grandpa, a few days will make a big difference. Once she's up and hopping around, she'll have less time to blame herself for being a nuisance to everyone — which is the way she feels now.'

'Well, thank you, Dr East.' I smiled round at him.

We arrived back at The Lodge to find the Parkers enthusing about their walk up Tall Hill, and an anxious Imogen waiting for news of Monica, especially because the Hale parents had phoned from Devon and she had promised to ring back. They were wondering whether to make the long jouney to visit the invalid.

'I said at least to wait till she gets home. There's nothing they can do, and

Daddy just can't cope with the travelling — '

'Very sensible, Imogen,' I approved.

There had been another call. Max had rung. Again.

'He's coming!' Imogen said dramatically. 'He's almost on his way! Probably a couple of days, he said. Looks like he can't wait to help us in our troubles — or at least, help you!'

'Good grief. Yes, that's what I was afraid of,' I muttered.

'Why aren't you interested in him? He sounds quite something.'

I made lame excuses, and slipped away up to my room. I had a letter to write. By now, surely, I deserved just a few minutes of this endless difficult day to myself.

For such a short letter — barely more than a single page — it took a long time to write to Damien. Partly that was because my fingers were shaking, and I kept reading and re-reading every line. I told him about Monica, about The Lodge. I hoped his work was progressing. I didn't mention Cecilia Brand. I didn't say the pain of our parting had never left me, that I missed him so deeply, despite all our differences I loved him still so much.

When the letter was sealed, even then I sat there holding it, tempted to tear it open again.

Thankfully, Imogen and Tim between them had got the children to bed. Even Barney was asleep, and Greg was leafing through old comics in his attic. I horrified Imogen by announcing, 'Good, now we can get to work!'

'Work? *Now?* You know, given time, you could be even worse to live with than Monica,' Imogen said weakly.

'Just a little gentle painting. And I need measurements for curtains. And I want to move some furniture. And there's the gift stall to organise . . . '

The long-suffering Parkers returned from an evening stroll to a strong atmosphere of wet paint. Tim and I between us made good progress. In fact, soon we were laughing quite immoderately about the collection of peculiarly gloomy, old paintings that must have come with the house — a couple of stern and bearded, old gentlemen apparently writing their wills, a shipwreck entitled 'Lost With All Hands', and a hook-nosed ballerina executing 'The Dying Swan'. He suggested we give the whole lot a double coat of Terra Cotta Haze.

'Surely not the Swan?' I objected. 'With all that dancing in her blood your Angel would never forgive us!' And since this looked like a unique chance I pressed, 'You never told me where in Paris your mother performed. I do know all the theatres quite well . . . '

I guessed this would be a signal for him to shut up like an especially ungregarious clam. Even Imogen's rampant curiousity, ever since his arrival, had elicited nothing about his background and his family — which caused her to hint darkly that the man must have something to hide.

This evening, I did achieve a minor breakthrough to impart to Imogen later. He told me briefly that as a fatherless young child he had been trailed round from second-rate stage door to stage door by his French dancer mother — billed simply as 'Marie-Angelique': and after she died at a tragically early age during a stay in England, he was brought up in a succession of orphanages. From these places he absconded more than once to live a hand-to-mouth existence on the streets. His one ambition now was to ensure Angel had proper training to develop her inborn talents.

A romantic story, a very sad story, I felt — with still some huge gaps in it, which he wasn't going to fill in a hurry. Wholly unmoved by my sympathetic interest — and my wistful mention that I, too, had lost my mother when only a child — he very hastily, very firmly, changed the subject.

Last thing, as the threatening rain clouds hadn't yet done their job, I stepped out into the warm scented night with a flashlight to water some new plants. And then again I was reduced to quite a helpless state of laughter — finding the two vultures on the gateposts were both wearing garlands of leaves round their necks and irreverent flowerpot hats on their heads.

Whatever the tragedies and traumas of Timothy East's shadowy life, none of them had quelled the spirit of mischief in him.

That Monday was just a beginning. Somehow the week moved along. The letter to Damien was posted, the café lurched from crisis to crisis, but business was improving — and my brightening-up ideas blossomed forth daily as I gained more confidence, and chivvied my fellow-workers into carrying them out.

Imogen had recovered from the first shock of Monica's accident and a vague sense of guilt about it, and now coped quite well with the children. Maybe she relied too often on lollipops all round and new comics or videos to keep them quiet, but I didn't question her methods.

I couldn't imagine what I would have done without Tim. We worked well together, we made a good team. Certainly I went out of my way to be friendly — he was so plainly a rolling stone, and it was vital he didn't get the urge to roll at present.

Nevertheless, Imogen's conviction that there was 'something odd about him' did surface once or twice. She came to me with some tale of finding him rooting around the cellar regions — and actually asking her if there was another way into them than the legitimate entrance door under the stairs.

'And is there?' I asked.

'I don't know! Possibly. But what business is it of his?'

As well, we both discovered Tim was a victim of severe insomnia. He slipped out for very late solitary strolls, or arose with the birds at the first glimmer of dawn to wander in the garden. For that, though, there seemed a credible explanation. What he called 'just headaches' could be something more serious. Finding him in a state of near collapse after some strenuous gardening, I flatly forbade him to do such heavy work for the present.

'I'm not an invalid,' he snapped at me. 'Mrs Hale wants the grounds done — '

'And Mrs Hale wouldn't want you doing them if you're not fit enough!'

Very nearly he gave me back an answer as forceful as it probably would be unrepeatable. This was not the only time.

As far as the gardens went, there was other help at hand. Maxwell Clyde arrived in person on the doorstep.

'He's here!' Imogen looked into the kitchen to tell me, when I was up to my elbows in late afternoon washing up. 'Maxwell Clyde — large as life and twice as handsome!'

'I'll be there in a minute,' I said.

'No hurry. I'll take him some tea. He doesn't need a room, he's staying at the Riverside Hotel — because he didn't want to put us to any trouble.'

Typical Max, I thought. A few minutes later I hurried outside. A few people were sampling our cream teas. At a far table beneath one of my new floral parasols Imogen was leaning on a chair, Barney draped over one shoulder. The man she was favouring with bright chatter looked round at me, his thin serious face full of concern, his gentle smile warm and welcoming.

'Lorraine. I'm so pleased to see you again.'

'How are you, Max?' I extended a hand that no longer boasted its long, carefully enamelled nails, brushing out of my eyes dark curly hair. 'You found us, then. What do you think of our set-up here?'

'He thinks it's fabulous, he was just saying,' Imogen said. 'I told him, it was nothing till you came!'

'Nonsense,' I deprecated. 'It's ninety per cent Monica's hard work.'

Max asked how she was, and I frowned over my answer. It was difficult to say how Monica was. She could hop around the ward now, but she didn't seem to want anything to do with the outside world. I found her either lethargic or ready to jump down my throat because Greg's hair looked unbrushed or Grandpa's creaking back was worse than usual. Everyone had been sworn to secrecy about the changes at The Lodge.

One other thing I had noticed was Tim's readiness to sit and chat to Monica. Obviously, he was grateful to her for giving him a job and a roof in somewhat unusual circumstances — and Monica, in her sharp, no-nonsense fashion, seemed equally ready to receive him. With Tim she was better tempered, more lively. Whatever all that meant, I wasn't as yet quite sure.

I gave Max some sort of summary of Monica's troubles. He had even more awkward questions to ask. Had I heard from Damien?

'As a matter of fact, yes. I believe he could be coming to England.' I glossed over that hastily, aware of the colour creeping into my face. 'Max, why have you booked in at the Riverside? Aren't we good enough for you here?'

'Simply because it isn't fair to take one of your rooms and give you extra work when I know you won't let me pay for it.'

'Of course I won't let you,' I agreed.

'I'm not here to be a nuisance, I'm here to help. Anything at all you need.'

Fortunately, I had given this some thought. I knew Max devoted himself whenever possible to his mother's large Derbyshire garden. He had shown me photos of it and the work he'd put in was tremendous.

'Well now, I do have a job that badly needs doing.' I waved a hand around the vista of grounds. 'See for yourself! Only the edges are presentable, the rest is primaeval jungle. Grandpa Hale is old and gets backache. Tim East — he's the helper Monica employed — has health problems. I'm not asking for miracles, but . . . '

He was looking around, his face brightening.

'Certainly I'll have a go at the garden. I'll start today if you like — '

'Tomorrow. Today, just take a look around and see where to start,' I suggested. This time, I had done things right on the tact and diplomacy count. I said truthfully, 'Well, that's a real weight off my mind!' — which made him look more pleased than ever.

I noticed, when I explained to Tim that Max would be helping in the garden, that the news was met with a dearth of enthusiasm. Perhaps he felt slighted that I had brought in a replacement gardener.

The very last thing needed at The Lodge were undercurrents or grudges! But I was really too busy to bother — and far more, a letter came for me that eclipsed all else, that lifted me to the stars.

Damien had answered by return. Amazingly soon after penning my letter to him, I held in my hands a sheet scribbled with his extravagant hand.

He missed me. He repeated that twice. He was pleased to have the very attractive photograph. He had just returned from seeing 'La Traviata', Maria Rosinelli was off-key, must be sickening for something . . .

I gave Miss Dunlop a cheque in lieu of notice, the scribble went on. *She turned out to be no earthly use. Now have a new secretary. Libby Somebody. None of them can hold a candle to you.*

I didn't know whether to laugh or cry. I couldn't stop shaking.

No final plans for coming to England, but I'm working on them. Look after yourself, he finished. *Don't work too hard. My respects to Mrs Hale, hoping she continues to improve.*

That was all. Except for the signature. *All my love — D.C.*

In the full-tilt rush of the morning, with busy clatterings from the kitchen, the buzz of Max's lawnmower, the squeak of brakes as Imogen returned from the 'school run', I stood there in a world of my own. I clutched the letter that so lately Damien's hands had held.

'Lorrie? Oh, there you are!' An excited Imogen burst in on me. 'Guess what they just told me at the hospital — they're thinking about Monica coming home! Maybe two or three days, Dr Radcliffe thinks — '

I murmured mechanically, 'Good.' It took a moment for her tidings to reach me. 'That's wonderful, Imogen!'

It was a day for good news. She looked utterly amazed when I seized both her hands and twirled her around like a whirligig.

4

'Here you are, Max!' I wended my way through a shaggy patch of shrubbery, armed with a tray of tea and cakes. 'Take five, that's an order! Or really you should be taking a couple of hours, you've been slaving here since early this morning — '

'This is a mammoth job, it needs a lot of work, but I'm enjoying it.'

So long as he was happy, that was something. He was getting plenty of fresh air in his lungs, eating good home cooking and quietly filling a useful place each day in our assorted household.

'Don't worry about me, I'm having a whale of a time!' he told me again now as he did every other time I brought him drinks or ices or an order to stop for lunch.

Nevertheless, my conscience wasn't

at all easy about Max. Eventually, there would be a day of reckoning to face.

In the meantime, he was obliged to slow down when we had a short spell of poorish weather, which produced varying effects on us all. We had two B & B bookings, one a family soaked in a shower, another couple enticed somehow by Tim. Fewer casual customers on walks and trips wandered in, but people who did come — especially the campers — wanted hot lunches. By now we had a reciprocal agreement with friendly Mrs Dawson-Blake at the riding stables that she displayed our poster and we hers, which brought us a few young girls in jodhpurs wanting drinks and snacks. My idea for a gift stall had prospered, and now filled attractively a corner of the indoor café, tempting people with cards, notepaper, guidebooks, all sorts of odds and ends.

With garden work delayed by the rain, Max was added to my willing/ unwilling work-force pushing ahead the indoor decorating and 'improvements'.

Also, he created a huge WELCOME HOME banner to decorate the doorway on the day of Monica's return. Her departure from the hospital was delayed, but that gave all the more time for preparations.

'Tomorrow!' Imogen finally told me, after an evening visit with Tim and Angel. 'Almost definitely. If Dr Radcliffe says OK, I can collect her about three.'

In a sudden, last-minute panic about Monica's homecoming, I had everyone running around putting things straight. Missing Tim, I sought him outside. It was an overcast evening, a breeze stirring the trees with a sound like a rushing tide as I hurried round to the rear regions, still very much in their overgrown state. At once I spotted Tim's fair head bent over something, and Max's garden spade reared against a wall.

'Tim, you're not doing the garden? Monica won't want to come home and find you collapsed!' I stormed at him in my concern. 'Anyway, you know this part is waiting till later, didn't you say yourself we should do 'the bits that show'?'

'Beg pardon, O Great Leader. Won't happen again.'

'Idiot,' I said companionably. 'Look, I'm glad I've caught you alone, there's something I want to say.'

'If it's about walking out on you, I'm still here, aren't I?'

'No, not that. It's Angel. You know early today I drove out to Belworth trying to get more of the paint that ran short? Well, I found this Academy of Dance, they take children from age three. It's run by a Madame Hortense Somebody. I collected a brochure — ' I rummaged it from my pocket, straightening the folds. 'Tap, ballroom, modern, ballet — the lot. Suppose I take Angel along for an entrance audition?'

Slowly he examined the leaflet, with its pictures of smiling little girls in tap-shoes or tutus. The last page had a note of tuition fees, and his forehead creased.

'I know,' I said quickly, 'it's pricey.' I struggled for tactful words that wouldn't give offence. 'Tim, I'm sure Angel has real talent. I'd love to contribute to the cost, it would be something really worthwhile. Won't you please think about it?'

'I've thought. It's kind of you, I appreciate it — ' The mobile hands gestured. 'I do have plans to get Angel proper training . . . but there's no sense in starting her off here, is there? We're just passing through. We'll soon be back in London or somewhere — '

'You will?' I muttered with a sense of dull disappointment. 'You're sure? She loves the countryside, she looks so much better than when she came.'

'She's nearly got over a bad case of Old Mother B-itis. The worst disease known to mankind.' He smiled at me, that bright playful smile of his that so transformed his face. 'Lorraine, thanks for bothering. But don't worry over Angel. I'll take good care of her, the best way I can.'

I nodded. I believed that, of course. A sense of impending loss still weighed upon me as we turned back to the house.

It was past midnight when I finally sought my bed, but I was awake again early to greet a beautiful clear sky. Even the weather had turned to help us celebrate the homecoming!

This was one day we really didn't need a roaring trade in the café — so of course, we were swamped with campers, walkers and car-trippers. At least it stopped anyone sitting around chewing their fingernails. Max was roped in to carry trays and take orders. At three o'clock, really much too early, Imogen and Grandpa drove off for the hospital, and I undertook to get the children into their pre-arranged clean outfits.

That was also much too early. Sarah, in sky-blue with pink ribbons, went digging for her newest pet worm in a freshly watered flower-trough. Greg, climbing a tree by the gate 'to spot the car coming', fell several feet to the ground — unhurt but sustaining ripped trousers and plenty of dirt. It was Barney, of course, who surpassed everyone: while Max's inexperienced back was turned in the kitchen Barney discovered a tray of eggs and experimented blissfully with dropping them one by one on the red-tiled floor to see which made the best explosion.

'Good grief!' I breathed inadequately, with visions of Monica arriving an hour before time. Max was deeply apologetic. Tim, always practical, had already produced mop and bucket.

'You handle the kids, Lorraine. I'll handle the mess. Angel, love, run this sandwich out to the joker in the fluorescent tracksuit. *Carefully.*'

She giggled delightedly at the chaos, bearing the plate outside with breathless care. She also helped quite a bit with washing mud from Sarah, raw omelettes from Barney, and plastering Greg's scraped knee.

It seemed only a moment later that Greg yelled, 'They're coming!

— they're here!'

Monica's old green Ford, with Monica inside it, was turning up the drive. Imogen was driving it quite sedately. On the back seat, beside an anxious Grandpa, I spotted my cousin's flaming-red hair and pale face.

Though I had so carefully rehearsed a reception committee for the invalid, of course it didn't work out that way. Greg was jumping about wildly, Sarah was in floods of tears. Barney, perched on Tim's shoulders when he spotted his mother, almost took a nosedive. In fact, Monica looked completely dazed by everything.

She must have felt like suddenly crowned royalty. She looked very small, very frail. As I opened the car door she was saying shakily, 'I don't understand — I — I don't know what's been happening here — '

Tim wheeled her inside to her specially prepared downstairs bedroom. Greg pranced ahead, with a still weepy Sarah. I escorted Grandpa who was suddenly feeling the strain.

'Lie down a while,' Tim ordered. 'Come on, no protests. You can see everything tomorrow. Tea, madame? Our home-baked wholemeal country scones, the speciality of the house . . . or something more substantial?'

'No. Just tea, I'm not hungry. Thank you, Tim,' she whispered.

She seemed loath to let go of his protective arm. Determinedly he was driving everyone from the room, rooting out Barney from under the bed and Greg from mountaineering on a tall bookcase.

A little later I carried in a tempting tea tray. It was my first moment alone with Monica. She declared still that she couldn't eat. To please me, she sipped the tea, her forehead wrinkled in a worried frown.

'Lorraine, it all looks wonderful, but — if you've been running up all sorts of bills — '

'No bills. I promise.'

'But — I don't understand, I just

couldn't possibly afford — '

'All taken care of.' I waved a hand to silence her. 'You see, I appointed myself a partner in The Lodge — this is my capital injection. I've enjoyed every minute of it! And when you're supervising a chain of executive hotels, well, certainly I won't mind taking my cut of the profits!'

'I don't want a hotel chain. I just want to know I'm paying my own way and not sponging on my relatives!' For the first time this sounded more like Monica.

'Please don't get upset. We've lots of time to discuss business,' I said.

Still frowning, she was surveying me in that disconcertingly direct way of hers. The pale piercing eyes behind their no-nonsense glasses were unchanged.

'And how are you, Lorrie? Any more news from the States?'

I was touched that, in the midst of everything, she still cared about my personal problems.

'Well, we've written. And talked on

the phone, and he never once mentioned Cecilia Brand. He's coming to England, I'm just waiting to hear the when.' I admitted, 'I just hope he doesn't take too long. I'm starting to look well past my sell-by date.'

I was amazed by her response. 'You've been working much too hard, I can't thank you enough — and don't worry, you look super. Like you always do.'

I told Monica quietly, the hard work was by no means all down to me. Imogen had helped well, Max had done wonders, even Grandpa. But it was Tim who had really worked himself into the ground. He had had a sad life, I added, basically he was a very caring person: most of all, he badly needed to put down some roots.

'I know,' Monica said. 'Yes, I know.'

I thought that she smiled to herself a little smile.

That outlandish scheme of mine for the future — her future and Tim's — was growing . . . and growing.

Inevitably, the euphoria of that homecoming day was impossible to maintain. There followed a difficult patch with Monica, in ways which I had never expected.

Mainly, of course, she was still very much an invalid, quite unable to take up the reins of the household. That meant she had to watch the rest of us doing in our own sweet way things she badly wanted to do herself — resulting, as she grew stronger, in many caustic comments and criticisms.

She seized on a paragraph in the local paper about a local 'prowler' alarming householders, and kept on saying it would have made more sense, instead of all the cosmetic improvements, to strengthen our security at The Lodge. As for the children, she considered they had been outrageously spoiled, showered with sweets, allowed to watch television at all hours. Et cetera, et cetera.

As though this wasn't provoking enough, another aspect left me not just annoyed, but devastated.

'It's no good asking *me*,' she would say when referred to about how she wanted a garden bed laid out, or today's menu, or whatever. 'Don't ask *me*, I'm just the owner here. I'll stay put in my room, so I won't be a nuisance to the staff.'

She had hailed my new ideas and innovations with a brusque, 'Very nice — pity I never had the time to think of it, or the money to spend on it.' She even said more than once, it was quite fortunate she had the disabling accident, allowing experts to take over her own bungling amateur efforts.

As far as Monica's difficult moods and acid tongue were concerned, another major sufferer was Imogen — who seemed to incur displeasure from the moment she crawled out of bed to the time her late-night call to Wayne was truncated by stern mention of the bill. But Imogen was immersed in private plans of her own, centred on her imminent birthday.

'I invited Wayne for the week-end. A sort of private dinner-party on Saturday, and Tim's promised to do the food . . . but what's the betting Mon won't allow it?'

'Oh, I'm sure she'll be delighted,' I assured her rashly. 'If she isn't, blame it on me, say I gave permission. Am I invited? I'm dying to see your Wayne!'

'Everyone's invited. Including you and your Max.'

I had despaired of convincing her that Max wasn't mine. In her eyes I was either being coy or I was just plain crazy: a shadowy presence over in the States ought to come a poor second.

At present Imogen seemed to be in a world of her own — and I sympathised, I whose heart leaped when the morning post arrived or the telephone rang. I did my best to smooth the way for her 'party'.

It happened that Monica had one of her follow-up hospital visits on the Friday and was very tired, so she didn't take too much notice of the arrangements. Saturday was sunny and beautiful. Quite early, an open blue sports car with a vicious-sounding engine zoomed up Abbots Lane.

'Wayne Forrester,' Imogen introduced me proudly. 'Wayne, this is my very good mate Lorraine. My — well, cousin-in-law, I suppose!'

'Hello, Wayne. Welcome to The Lodge! I've heard so much about you.' I offered him a welcoming hand.

'Imogen,' I instructed her, 'you're certainly not working on your birthday, so you and Wayne go out and enjoy yourselves, I'll square it for you here! Just mind you're back by six for the celebration!'

The hardest thing was to keep an almost drooling Greg away from the blue car and prevent him clambering in with them.

Naturally, everyone who came into the café today seemed to have been fasting for weeks and determined to make up for it. Max's efforts to help weren't too successful, until he bore all four children well clear of the hectic scene to keep them amused. Monica rested on a shady patch of lawn, attended by Grandpa. Tim and I, red-faced and damp-haired, in shorts and T-shirts, laboured mightily. It was odd that I had a weird sense of enjoyment in the midst of overheating and overwork — helped on its way by Tim's cheery comments.

Somehow, by the evening, everything was under control. The table in the dining room was resplendent with a white cloth and best china. All of us gathered around very similarly arrayed in our best, with Monica at the foot and Imogen tonight at the head. There were cards and gifts galore from the Hale parents in Devon, and the Forrester parents, and various friends and all of us besides.

I sat beside Max, who looked rather wistfully pleased at being part of the cheery family gathering. The one absentee was Tim, who insisted on doing all the work, but he was present for the highlight of the occasion, doubtless planned for later but embarked upon before the meal even began.

'Wayne, let's do it now!' Imogen was nudging him vigorously. 'Ladies and gentlemen and children — and kitchen hands,' she nodded across at Tim. 'This is an announcement! We're going to . . . we're getting . . . we're engaged!' She got the word out finally. 'And we've bought the ring today! Come on, Wayne, what are we waiting for?'

In front of all of us he produced a jewellers' box and self-consciously slipped a diamond on to her finger. Imogen sparkled as much as the jewel, her bronze hair floating around the shoulders of a summer-blue dress that matched her bright eyes. Wayne kissed her in demure fashion fit for the public gaze. The room buzzed with laughter and congratulations.

Especially, I was pleased that Imogen first of all trotted round to show her ring to Monica, and that Monica was smiling quite brightly. Her brusque reminder, 'Mind you take it off when you wash up,' set everyone laughing again. She added, 'You're much too young, of course, but you're a good girl, Imogen — I'm pleased for you both, I hope you'll be very happy together.'

There was a passing wistfulness in the words of the young widow, but no more than that. She put an arm round Imogen with a brief warm squeeze.

I sat there watching the happy scene, so welcome after the stress of these past weeks. I joined in the merry toasts. This was a joyous day, romance was in the air! If Damien had been here beside me it would have been perfect . . .

But in Damien's continued absence my thoughts could stray along a tangent, that wild idea born in my mind over these past few days. A new man in Monica's life could transform her whole saddened and darkened world. Someone to love and cherish her, to understand and comfort her lasting grief . . . someone to be a new father to her children, to share the responsibilities that burdened her solitary shoulders and bring again sunlight to her empty skies . . .

Was the answer not obvious? With my own eyes I had seen her special liking for Tim, her trust in him, her readiness for his company even at bad moments. I had watched, too, Tim's eagerness to help her, his understanding, his liking and respect for her. Surely it was providential that he had arrived on her doorstep when both of them were in sore need! And wouldn't this solve not their problems alone, but magically transform the short sad life of little Angel?

If I could play matchmaker for them, I would do it with all my strength, with highest hopes! There was just one proviso, before I could be wholly happy about Monica's involvement in the East family, it was vital now, to clear up to my own satisfaction the mysteries shrouding Tim's unknown past.

And there was no time like the

present! The festive table was still abuzz with chatter and laughter after Imogen's bombshell news. I mumbled something unintelligible and slipped from my chair. No-one would miss me.

At the top of the house was the big attic in which Tim had set up temporary home. An archway divided off part of it, where Angel's bed was installed, surveyed regally by two wall posters of Pavlova and Fonteyn. With great guilt, though my intentions were the best in the world, I started opening drawers, peering into the wardrobe, getting down from on top of it Tim's battered suitcase.

Inside that, my shaky hands came upon a carrier-bag full of mementos of other days. There were much handled stage photographs of 'Marie-Angelique', Tim's mother, with piled up hair, flashing dark eyes, long earrings, a flounced gown with a corsage of flowers ... most remarkable of all, her facial resemblance to Angel. There were old programmes, letters, baby pictures, a wedding photo of a younger, strangely serious-faced Tim with a pretty dark-haired girl. Another portrait of the same girl in neat nurse's uniform was inscribed, 'To Darling E from your loving J'. I stood there staring at it. 'E' . . . 'Darling E' . . . ? Why would Tim's wife inscribe this picture to him like that? . . .

There were sounds on the stairs. Somehow I bundled the things away, heaved the suitcase back into place. There was no chance to escape from the room.

'Hello!' a voice exclaimed in surprise.

It was only Angel. My heart was still racing. I wouldn't make a good burglar.

'Hello,' I responded. 'I was just — looking around for something that might be in here . . . Is the party breaking up yet?'

'No. No, it's not. I just thought I'd go to bed.'

Her voice sounded small and forlorn. Of course, the party below wasn't her family. I understood that.

'Angel, tell me something. Do you remember your mummy?'

'A bit. She was a nurse, she had a blue dress. Watches and scissors on it . . . '

'That's right. And where did you live with Mummy?'

'It was a flat. No garden. We had a goldfish, but it died.'

'And — ' I probed gently. 'What happened to Mummy?'

'It was the fire, wasn't it? There was lots of smoke and crackles — I kept on choking because I couldn't breathe, only someone saved me . . . '

The quiver of the little girl's mouth tore at my heart. Following on this desperate loss must have come her father's serious car accident, his long spell in hospital which consigned Angel to the care of strangers.

Impulsively, I sat down on her bed and opened my arms. She clung round my neck, her tears wet against my cheek.

'I'm sorry I asked you, sweetheart,

don't think about it any more,' I whispered.

* * *

'Drama, folks!' Imogen announced, waving the local newspaper above our early morning breakfast table. Listen to this! 'THE PHANTOM PROWLER STRIKES AGAIN!' — '

Following her wonderful week-end, she had spent most of Monday recovering. This was Tuesday, the day of the School Fête and Sports at Greg and Sarah's school. Imogen, downing coffee in her bathrobe, claimed our attention.

'Listen. 'After reports of a shadowy prowler gaining access to outbuildings and gardens in the leafy Abbots Lane area the intruder was finally glimpsed late on Sunday evening by frail elderly widow Mrs Edith Carne of The Birches, who heard noises in her cellar and bravely went to investigate. She subsequently collapsed with the shock and was taken to the Memorial

Hospital. Police say nothing appears to be missing from the premises, probably because Mrs Carne surprised the intruder who immediately fled the scene . . . '

'Did you say The Birches?' I reflected.

'The next house along. Their grounds back on to our wall!' Imogen pointed out. 'Too close for comfort, eh? We'd better chain down the café tables and padlock the bird bath!'

Grandpa muttered that things were coming to a pretty pass when law-abiding citizens couldn't feel safe in their own beds. In fact, since Monica had spotted hints of this previously, he had taken to checking all our locks and bolts several times each evening. His pernickety fumblings had been driving me mad — but this fresh newspaper story was disquieting. As Imogen put it, 'too close for comfort.'

She was reading with relish the words of Mrs Carne, who it seemed suffered from a heart problem and was staying in hospital for observation: ''He was just a shadow moving in a corner, I thought my last moment had come . . . ' Don't know why she says *he* when it was just a shadow, couldn't it have been a prowleress?'

By now I was hardly listening. Imogen had planted the newspaper in front of Tim, who had just come in, telling him brightly, 'Read all about the poor old lady floored by the dreaded Phantom! — Feel like volunteering for the Abbeybridge Vigilantes, Tim?'

She wasn't looking at Tim, too busy pouring more coffee, but I was looking at him. Unmistakably, I saw every vestige of colour drain from his face. I saw the urgency with which he read the paragraph. For that unguarded instant he looked a desperately hounded man, a sick man . . . a guilty man.

The next moment he was telling Imogen, rather shakily, 'OK, count me in for the Vigilantes! . . . ' He seemed to forget all about breakfast and walked out.

I went on sitting there, my mind

racing with unreal horror. I had seen what I had seen. It was no dream. Tim, with all his closely kept secrets, his unpredictable moods and nocturnal wanderings, *could* he be this 'prowler'? I knew he was a sick man, but how sick was he really? What strange form might that sickness, his disabling 'headaches', take?

I drove the monstrous idea away, but it wouldn't stay away. And there followed on another wild imagining, no less horrifying. When old Mr Hale bolted us securely in at night — was he keeping the 'prowler' out or fastening him in?

Oh, the whole thing was incredible, it had to be! And yet, how to work beside Tim that day and behave as normal, I wasn't at all sure. As it happened, this was an abnormal day altogether, with the school events dominating the scene. Monica had wanted to go, but after a poor night was tired and fretful: it was arranged that Tim would keep The Lodge going with Max and Mr Hale, so

Imogen and I could attend at the school fête — taking along Barney and Angel, money for the stalls, a camera, and our voices ready to cheer the sports winners.

'Sure you won't come, Monny?' Imogen asked as we were ready to leave.

'No, you don't want to be bothered with me. I'll stay here.'

'I'll look after her,' Tim assured us. 'Don't forget to drop around a few of our 'Abbeybridge Cream Teas' leaflets!'

The smile I tried to give him was rather a shaky one.

I couldn't recall when last I attended an occasion like this. It wasn't part of Damien's world, so hadn't been part of mine.

Part of the field was roped into measured areas and presently the sports got started. We cheered Greg madly, and stopped cheering when he fell over a couple of yards short of the tape. We were wrapped in embarrassment when Sarah remained static at the shout of

'Go!' and then burst into tears.

Midway through was an interval when a 'Visitors Talent Contest' took place. 'Angel,' I persuaded her, 'this is for you, go for it, girl!' She didn't need much coaxing, queueing with me eagerly at the 'signing-on' table.

'One for the Under Sevens,' I told the teacher in charge. 'She'd like to dance — but how about music?'

'Mrs Evans can play mostly anything on her portable keyboard. Will you write the name on this entry form? Or can you do it, dear?' she asked Angel.

Angel nodded importantly. In a large round hand I watched her write: Angelique WEST.

For a moment I stood there transfixed at this strangest of mistakes. It was Imogen who started laughing and teasing, 'Goodness, child, don't you know yet whether you're an East or a West? Sure you're not a North or a South?'

She kept on laughing after Angel had

hastily scratched out the words and corrected it. I wasn't laughing at all. I had seen the way Angel clapped an anxious hand to her mouth when she realised her mistake. Or was it a horrified and frightened hand?

I just hoped this strange incident wouldn't put her off her dancing — and it didn't. Asked for 'Swan Lake', Mrs Evans asked, 'Do you mean this?' — and capably produced a few familiar bars. Among the rather sparse Under-Sevens entries — an inaudible song or two, a jerky recitation, some wobbly cartwheels from a young gymnast — Angel's contribution was in another class. The audience was suddenly stilled, passing people paused to watch: the inborn grace of the little girl, raptly living the music, light as thistledown in her impromptu display, was a glimpse of pure natural beauty.

It was no surprise, at the end of the prizegiving, for the head teacher to announce through her megaphone, 'The Under-Sevens Visitors Talent

Contest . . . By a unanimous vote from our judges, the winner is . . . Angelique East. Will you come up here for your prize, Angelique? — Very well done! . . . '

'Go on, Angel! — go on!' I pushed her forward and whipped the camera into action as she received a paintbox amid warm applause, and her hand was gravely shaken by the 'judges'.

On the way home, Angel happily clutched her prize, delighted with her success but still, I believed, upset over her mistake with the name. The car had scarcely stopped at The Lodge before the children were tumbling excitedly out, their arms full of things from the stalls and a warm and weary bag of sweets for their mother. Barney still resembled a sugary sunset.

It was Max who received us, with the obvious comment, 'So you all had a good time?'

'Brilliant!' Greg pranced boisterously.

I was asking with anxiety, 'How did you manage with the café, Max?'

'Oh, we managed. We did have some excitement here. The police came in giving us the third degree, not very good for our image!'

I felt my blood run cold. I whispered, 'The police?'

'Just asking about this prowler scare, if we'd ever seen or heard anything. Of course, we couldn't really help. Then there was a phone call for you, Lorraine. Damien is coming to London next week, I took down his flight details. He wants you to book him a hotel and a car.'

'He wants me — ' I echoed dully. 'Doesn't Libby do his bookings?'

'He's already got rid of her.' He was looking very seriously into my face. 'I told him you don't work for him any more, he has no right to impose on you — '

'Oh.' I waved a hand. 'I'll do it, no problem. But . . . '

Although the longed for news had come at last, I couldn't take it in. My mind was too full of its other problems.

'Tell me,' I asked shakily, 'did the police speak to Tim? What happened? Oh, I wish I'd been here . . . '

Out of the corner of my eye I saw Tim beside Monica's chair on the lawn. I badly needed to talk to someone. Not Monica, of course, she mustn't be unduly worried — and most of all I shrank from sowing seeds of probably unfounded suspicion and spoiling a growing relationship . . .

Like an answer from the blue I looked up at the man beside me. I floundered, 'Max, I've got a terrible problem. I — I don't know what to do about it . . . '

5

It was a little later that I managed a private talk with Max. We sat together on that secluded stone bench in the rear gardens where more than once I had talked to Tim. At present, I was glad Tim was busy elsewhere.

'Say whatever you want,' Max prompted. 'It's Damien, isn't it?'

I shook my head. 'No, it's not Damien. Max, this is something quite different, you're going to send for the men in white coats when I tell you. I'm wondering — if Tim could be the prowler!'

It was his turn to look utterly startled. 'What? Tim? *Our* Tim?'

'Our Tim. There's plenty of evidence. Let me try to explain . . . '

I did my best to outline that evidence clearly and logically. The head injuries that could have caused unknown harm:

the 'insomnia' and nocturnal wanderings; Tim's evasion of all personal questions, his striking reaction to the newspaper, his odd interest in derelict corners and cellars. The photograph strangely inscribed 'To Darling E', and perhaps equally Angel's unguarded signature, 'Angelique *West*' . . .

'He could be staying here under an assumed name. He could be anybody! There might be all sorts of things on his conscience, that's why he's skulking here in the country, where no-one knows him — with his wrap-around sunglasses as a mask, he probably even wears them in the bath . . . '

Max listened attentively.

'It does seem to hang together. I can see why you're so worried. But — ' He frowned doubtfully. 'Circumstantial evidence can be very damning, and it can also collapse if one new piece is added. Would you like me to ask him about it? Or both of us ask him together?'

'How can we do that? — when it's probably all rubbish, and he'll be furious and walk out, and — Monica will be very upset?'

'All right. That leaves only two alternatives. We must watch him like hawks, try to think up traps he might fall into . . . or we can go to the police,' he suggested soberly. 'That's what we really should do.'

'No,' I muttered, 'not the police. Not yet. Who knows, meantime they might catch the real prowler — think what fools we'd look then!'

'I'm not bothered about that. I'm more bothered about the safety of the household. And other people's households, of course . . . '

Max was very kind, very sensible, so eager to help me. I felt just a little better for knowing I wasn't facing this impossible problem alone. Indeed it was true that, always blinded by Damien, I had never appreciated Max nearly enough . . .

Indoors, the talk was largely about the school fête — and also a new B & B couple who had just booked in.

'Saw them plodding up the lane with enormous back-packs,' Tim explained, 'so I convinced them they needed a night's unbounded luxury in our first floor front.' He grinned at me across the table.

Not a prowler's grin, not in a million years!

And yet, mindful of Max's counsel, I spent a wretched night propping my eyelids open, listening for a footfall or a creaking door. I heard neither, only the distant reverberations of Grandpa's snore. The B & B's, next door to him, might be wishing they had unloosed their bed-rolls in the whispering woods.

Arising in the morning, a sudden blinding light broke through to me. Damien would be in London this week — three days from now! Until this moment, I hadn't quite realised. In haste I arranged his bookings. I made myself a hair appointment, also a manicure. I dashed into the town for new shoes, and a stylish, slim-skirted pale blue summer suit I spotted in a boutique.

Returning from the hairdresser's I found I had missed another minor excitement. Someone had miscalculated that deceptive bend in the lane and driven into the tail-end of our lengthy wall, breaking their lights and uprooting a venerable brick or two.

'A bad spot, that,' Mrs Dawson-Blake observed. 'That curve needs a warning sign or something. We don't want another smash like the one before. A bad storm it was, and pitch dark, and this poor young chap — probably on holiday and going much too fast, but he must have lost control and . . . wham!'

'Wham?' I echoed with suitable awe.

'The car looked like a burned-out concertina, Mr Carne said, and the driver was critical, they had to transfer him to some specialised hospital — I never did know what happened to him, crippled for life I daresay . . .'

That same evening, just after the café shut, I came upon a distressed Sarah who poured out some confused talk about Cousin Herbert, her newest worm friend. She led me to a flowerbed, where Tim must have been supervising Herbert's domiciliary arrangements. A spade and a jar lay on the grass, and Tim was crumpled beside them like a man in grave pain.

'We were just moving Herbert,' Sarah wailed, 'and — and — '

'All right, precious. Run inside and tell Auntie Gen to come,' I told her. I dropped on to the grass to cushion Tim's head gently in my lap.

'Tim, you'll be all right,' I whispered. I stroked the fair hair from his damp taut forehead. 'We'll get a doctor, don't try to move . . . '

Imogen was hastening over the grass with a glass of water.

'Gee whiz! What happened?' she asked. 'Timothy, have you been eating some of your own food?'

'He passed out,' I said seriously. 'And I'm sure it's not the first time, and it won't be the last. Imogen, you try talking some sense into him!'

It was the very next day, Friday, that Imogen and I engineered for him a break from the café. A circus was in town, where its big top had blossomed on the river green. The school term had been over two whole days, and already Greg was finding life at The Lodge deadly dull and Sarah was drooping about the place with ants or woodlice in jars — not conducive to improving the customers' appetites.

'I've booked some seats for the five o'clock show!' I announced. 'Three adults, three children. Shall we draw straws, or — '

'No need,' Imogen said obligingly. 'I'll stay home with Monny and Grandpa. The clowns might frighten Barney — or maybe he'd frighten them? So, you and Tim and Max take the other three kids. And good luck!'

Tim wasn't enthusiastic, but Angel was so delighted that he couldn't back out.

Greg was vastly disillusioned to find

there would be no animals on show.

He sat between Max and myself and cheered up at the clowns' slapstick, the jugglers, the trapeze fliers. On my other side was Tim, next to him an enraptured Angel. She leaned across to tell me the Trapeze Queen's cloak of satin and sequins was beautiful, and it probably wasn't *too* hard to somersault in the air.

'Beware,' I whispered to Tim, 'Madame Hortense's ballet class is one thing, we don't really want any fancy flying notions!'

He made a wry face at the idea. He was laughing, seeming to enjoy the show through his little daughter's eyes. Everything was fine until the second half, when we watched some acrobats and trick cyclists: then followed a grim exhibition of sword-swallowing — which had Sarah's face hidden tightly against Max — and fire-eating. Two muscular young men in loincloths bathed their bare bodies with flaming torches before plunging the flares down their throats.

'Not to be tried at home,' I warned Greg. Then I realised that another member of our party was enjoying this even less than Sarah.

Tim sat beside me as though turned to stone. I could see his forehead glistening wet, his face drained of colour. I thought of his young dark-haired wife, Angel's mother — and impulsively, forgetful of all else, I reached for his hand.

For a moment it clung fast to mine. I sat very still.

'Sorry,' Tim said suddenly, and got to his feet. 'See you outside!'

The hand tore from mine.

'Shall I come with you?' I asked.

'No. Just — look after Angel.'

Then he was gone, people craning and muttering as he pushed past them.

I turned to look at Max. 'Did you see his face?' I whispered.

'I did. Yes, I think you're right,' Max answered softly. 'He's a haunted man.'

Whatever else the show contained, I

scarcely knew. Outside, in the home-going throng, Tim joined up with us again.

'Sorry about that! The tent was too warm.' he apologised without flames and furnaces to boot.'

Back at The Lodge, Greg and Angel poured out accounts of the show over the family meal. Afterwards, Tim started a major baking operation to replenish our depleted stocks. I wanted very much to join him, to beg him to confide in me things I could only guess and things I dared not imagine . . .

But for once I didn't rush in where angels feared to tread. For once, I had no earthly idea what to say or how to say it.

I went quite early to bed. In just a few hours, Damien would be in London.

The phone call came about two in the afternoon. I took it in the public hallway, for once quite private, but in fact the conversation was brief.

The room at the Beverley and the

hired car were fine, Damien said. But then I always was reliable with bookings — unlike some others. He was fine, too, except he had urgent letters to write and meetings to fix. He was looking forward to seeing me. Would I come to his hotel tomorrow?

I would. Of course I would. Clearly he had arrived alone, because the hotel reservation was in one name only.

As for whether I was summoned as a secretary acting and unpaid, an old friend — or something more than a friend — was rather less clear.

'My boss,' I told Tim succinctly in the kitchen. 'At least, the man I used to work for — years and years, all around the world. He's a music critic and author. Did you ever hear of Damien Clyde?'

'Nope! Not really my scene. Oh, I've started the last pack of pizzas?'

I nodded. 'I'm meeting him in London tomorrow. I could possibly stay over till Monday, he has a lot of work to get through . . .'

'Right. Can you run this jug of hot water out to the couple with the bawling baby, so they can warm up a bottle?'

'Yes,' I said rather flatly, disappointed by his lack of interest.

With a few overnight oddments in a small suitcase I set out just as the café opened. Max ran me into town. It was strange to be walking out on The Lodge — the place had filled my life every day since I arrived here. I would have deserted it for no other reason than Damien.

'Nice of you to bother, Max,' I told him at the station.

'No bother,' he said bleakly. 'Have a good time.'

The London train was due in, and I was glad. This was all very difficult.

The rail journey seemed strangely unreal, watching the countryside slip past the windows as I watched it a while ago when I travelled to The Lodge unsure what to expect, what reception I would get. The interval dividing the two journeys, those busy crowded weeks, was suddenly like a hazy dream.

The big London terminus was crowded. I managed to get a taxi and requested, 'Beverley Hotel, please.'

The Beverley wasn't much of a landmark, a grey, square, staid-looking building that had stood for aeons on the edge of the West End. Marching through its doorway, I rehearsed what I would say at Reception. 'I'm Miss Harrison, I have an appointment with Mr Damien Clyde . . . '

There was no need to say anything. 'Lorraine,' a voice hailed me quietly.

I turned, and he was there.

'Damien. Hello again,' I heard a voice say. It must have been my voice. I looked up into the face that had haunted my waking and sleeping. 'Did — did you have a good journey?'

I didn't even hear what he answered, or if he answered.

Used as I was to my recent association with Max, the likeness of the brothers struck me anew . . . and hazily I noted that Damien's dark hair was lightly silvered at the temples, his eyes were a little less blue, his more aquiline features a little less regular.

'You look well.' he was saying. Those eyes were taking in the new slimmer me, my pink-faced confusion, the pale-blue suit. I was glad of the suit, and the hair-do, and the manicure.

'It — it must be all the hard work,' I explained. 'You'd never believe what we all get through in a day. I can't quite believe it myself!'

'I'm glad you've arrived because I was just dashing out — I was going to leave a message for you. Olaf Peterssen's new Symphony is being premiered this afternoon at the Festival Hall — remember we spent a day with Olaf in Berlin? He just sent me round a couple of tickets. Will you come?'

'Oh. Yes!' I agreed.

'We'll just have time for a drink and a chat with Olaf before the performance. Afterwards I'm seeing Gertrude Melier at her flat, she's discovered some more ancient concert programmes she thinks will interest me. Anything like the last mouse-eaten lot and they won't! Afterwards we can have dinner somewhere in peace, I've lots to discuss with you. What do you say?'

'Yes!' I said lamely. It seemed as though in one instant I had been whisked back in time and dumped straight into a life I thought was gone for ever.

I still stood there rather awkwardly holding my small suitcase. I hesitated, 'You sounded as though you had a lot of work to do, so — '

'So you can stay over? Good! Fix yourself up with a room — charged to me, of course — and you may want to freshen up, London's hideously hot and dusty, but be ready to leave in ten minutes sharp. Even that will be cutting it a bit fine.'

I was ready in nine minutes and thirty seconds.

Olaf Peterssen, tall and very blond, chatted to us volubly in a sing-song

Swedish accent over drinks at the Festival Hall. Beyond the building's glass façade, the wide sun-flecked tideway of the Thames rippled and sparkled lazily. In the impressive auditorium we had a box, Damien and I. He scribbled his largely illegible notes, gold half-lensed glasses slipping down his nose. There was something about the unfortunate conductor that seemed to rile him.

'He's missing the point entirely. Olaf should have taken the baton himself. This young what's-his-name is just perched there like a vacant penguin — '

'Will you put that in your review, Mr Clyde?' I giggled quite uncontrollably.

'If the fancy takes me, Miss Harrison. Hush please!'

Momentarily he giggled, too. I remembered vividly other similar times; on these occasions, when he was so far from the arrogant, difficult man who had aroused in my heart a rending love/hate passion, there was room only for love.

On magical rapid wings the after-noon flew by. After the concert there was Gertrude Melier's claustrophobic geranium-scented flat.

The henna-tinted lady welcomed us warmly with camomile tea and ginger biscuits. She had supplied Damien with helpful material for his books and articles a couple of times.

Today she produced a bundle of frayed programmes, and a few old theatre magazines. Sipping the herbal brew — with a sideways glance at me of acute distaste — Damien selected a few, and penned a cheque.

It was strange, but for the first time I thought back to The Lodge — and even now, it wasn't Monica or the Sunday café trade I remembered. Those old programmes had stirred a vivid recol-lection.

'Damien, did you ever hear of Marie-Angelique? A dancer in Paris and thereabouts, it would be — oh, maybe twenty-five or thirty years ago — ' I asked.

'What did she do?'

'I'm not too sure. Can-cans in backstreet night-clubs, probably. But she was in a few stage shows. It's just that — I know her granddaughter.'

He said he would bear the name in mind. With him, that didn't mean too much. His mind, every moment of his waking day, were excessively crowded.

It was hard to escape from Miss Melier, but we managed finally. It was a calm, cool evening. At last we had some time to ourselves, in an Italian restaurant, with vases of fragrant crimson roses, candles in chianti bottles, we ate and talked.

'Well, now,' Damien said, 'this is nice. Lorraine, I've missed you. Very much.'

'You really missed me? Even with — er — Marsha, and Libby — ' I said softly.

'Libby was a disaster. Marsha was an imbecile masquerading as a secretary. No, I needed *you*. You know that, don't you? And not just because you can type more than twenty words per minute and spell, and placate people when I upset them — Shall we try the zabaglione?'

'Well, I shouldn't. All right!' I had to agree. 'We don't actually serve that at my cousin's café! — '

'Ah yes, this café. I was impressed by the picture. Tell me all about it.'

We lingered on as the evening grew later, sipping more wine, talking and talking. About Monica, Imogen, the big old house, the assorted children. About Max and his new job beginning in the Autumn. About next week-end, when Damien planned to run up to Derbyshire to see his mother.

This seemed an endless day, yet I had never been less tired, I wanted it to go on and on. Before we left, Damien had some news that transcended all else.

'I'm planning to stay in London a few weeks, certainly not more — then I've a major new project lined up. I've been waiting to tell you.'

'You're leaving the country again?' I said dully.

'That's right. I'm travelling East. Japan, China, possibly Tibet . . . I've been commissioned to do a book on the Musical Culture of the whole region — a subject I know nothing about, I kept very quiet about that. So it'll need a mountain of research. Especially on-the-spot investigation. How do you feel about it?'

'How do *I* feel . . . ?' I echoed. The inference seemed obvious, but I was taking nothing for granted. 'You're asking me — ?'

'To come with me. Please! Oh, yes, we've had our differences — if they were my fault, accept my humble apologies. It took you walking out on me to demonstrate how much I need you. I can't face doing this trip alone . . . '

'I didn't walk out, I've told you before. I gave you fair notice,' I muttered. The one question he hadn't attempted to answer hung heavily in the air between us. I had to give it voice. 'Damien, why would you go alone when you could take Miss Brand along?'

'Cecilia?' He waved one of those slender hands quite casually. 'No, no! She's attending the Music Festival in Canada . . . I'm not exactly sure where she is at this moment, but she's performing in Montreal next month . . . '

How could he sound so incredibly vague about Cecilia Brand — if he loved the woman half as much as I loved him? His eyes were looking straight into mine, robbing me of clear thought. His hand picked up mine from the table and held it lightly, his touch a caress that whirled all my senses into unbelieving joy.

'Just the two of us, Lorraine. No-one else to cramp our style. We'll have a lot of work to get through — but it won't be all work. We had some good times in the past didn't we? I promise you, this will be the best yet . . . '

Was it some sort of pride, or purely instinctive caution about being hurt all over again, that made me delay my answer? I said weakly I would 'think about it.' We left the restaurant, and outside the pavements were quiet and cool under a great milky moon, pale and ghostly, challenging the garish electric lights.

He hadn't brought his car, but in his usual fashion he had only to lift a hand and a taxi materialised at the kerb. Inside, we sat close together. The lighted façade of the Beverley received me. He suggested we have another drink, but I shook my head.

'I'm rather tired. For weeks now I've been used to early, early bedtimes and early, early mornings!'

Damien shuddered dramatically at the very thought. He said gently, 'Then you get some rest, you deserve it. But first — when will you have an answer for me? I need to know, I've a lot of planning to do.'

I should have remembered, of course, he was the most impatient man on God's earth. I said quietly, 'I'd like to sleep on it, Damien. Do you mind?'

'Of course not. Whatever you think best.' Was there just the tiny beginning of irritation in his voice?

'But you'd still like to come to Japan with me,' Damien's voice insisted softly. 'Wouldn't you, Lorraine? We would have such a marvellous time.'

In all honesty, all else besides, I had to admit, 'Yes. Yes, I would like to.'

He didn't kiss me good-night. Perhaps that was wholly my fault, I broke quickly away from him — or I would be able to make no lucid decisions at all. I sought my room, where the little suitcase I packed this morning — it seemed an age ago — awaited me.

If ever there was to be a night when sleep was impossible, despite this expensive and quietly opulent room Damien had provided, I faced it now.

6

It was past noon, the next day, before I left London. During the morning I had made phone calls, fixed meetings, typed rushed letters on the familiar portable machine I never thought to use again. Almost effortlessly I slipped back into my old role — but there was a change. Damien was charm and consideration itself. Jekyll and Hyde had turned to pure Jekyll.

That afternoon Damien was driving just north of London to meet up with his publisher for a round of golf and a business discussion. His offer to deliver me down to Sussex first was, of course, not meant to be accepted.

'Completely the wrong direction. Just drop me near a station,' I insisted.

He threaded through the lunchtime traffic with a nonchalance that made it look easy. There was no chance for lengthy farewells as he pulled into a kerb.

'I'll ring you,' he said, and in another moment his car had been swallowed up. I stood alone with my suitcase by the station forecourt.

It didn't matter that this was a stopping train, it just gave me precious time to catch my breath. My mind was in a whirl because still I hadn't given Damien my final answer. A dozen times today it had risen to my lips and slipped away unspoken. Of course, he seemed to be taking it as settled that the answer was 'Yes' — and why not, indeed? I had dealt efficiently with his paperwork, filled up dates in his diary — but something far less vague was needed to set me checking over my passport and sorting out flights for a very major journey.

I should have given him my answer! Why hadn't I seized instantly on this wonderful chance to start again along a road I thought closed for always?

Almost too soon Abbeybridge Station, basking in the afternoon sun, received me home — except it wasn't really my home, it was Monica's. Today there was no obliging car to meet me. That meant a bus, and an uncomfortable trudge on my elegant high heels.

My first glimpse of The Lodge should have been enough to convince me I was no longer indispensible here. A reasonable afternoon clientele sprinkled the pleasant café garden, waited upon cheerily by Imogen in a bright T-shirt lettered COME AND GET IT. Max in the background was tending lawns he had already somehow turned from unkempt meadowland into green velvet. Grandpa sat under a tree showing Barney and Sarah a picturebook. All of them marked my return with a decidedly casual wave.

Indoors, the same impression was even stronger. Greg was glued to a video, Angel tinkering on the piano. In the big kitchen, most amazingly Monica was back in charge! — or at least, overseeing operations from a stool.

'Oh, it's you,' she said. 'We didn't expect you till later — did we, Tim? How was London?'

'Fine!' I strove to be equally casual. 'So you've been managing here?'

'No problem,' Tim replied. 'Plus we had a B & B couple book in. Over the top health freaks — jogging before breakfast, organic muesli, and why hadn't we installed a swimming pool when we had space outside going spare. Dead weird, weren't they, Monny?'

'Maybe not so weird,' she countered. 'Didn't you say a pool would be a good attraction for visitors? So long as I get someone else to dig the hole?'

They laughed together. They looked curiously at home working side by side. It occurred to me, rather hurtfully, it had taken my brief absence to get Monica involved again instead of feeling sorry for herself in her sickroom.

'I'll get changed and give you a hand, shall I?'

Monica quashed that in her direct way. 'We don't need a hand just now. Did you have lunch?'

'Oh — ' For a moment I wasn't even sure about that. 'No, but I'm not hungry.'

'Nonsense,' my forcefully sharp-tongued cousin said. 'Go outside and sit yourself down. Just give Imogen an order.'

I opened my mouth and shut it again.

I settled down quite peacefully to sip my coffee and listen idly to the chatter from the next table.

A brief respite of peace it proved to be. The voices intruded more and more.

'A police car . . . ' — 'No, *two* police cars . . . ' — 'And how about poor old Mrs Carne, look what it did to her . . . ' — 'In the middle of the night again . . . '

I turned quickly to ask, 'There hasn't been another prowler scare?'

There had been. The night before, almost on our doorstep. Another resident spotting a nocturnal visitor, another disused outbuilding ransacked — and a man's footprint in a newly watered flowerbed, so this woman had heard from the boy who delivered papers by bicycle along Abbots Lane. 'That'll give them something to go on,' she said confidently, 'with all this forensic science they've got nowadays they'll soon arrest someone, you'll see! And the sooner the better. It gives you the creeps having this lunatic around . . .'

The sun was as warm, the sky was as blue. I went on sitting there. It was only a few moments before Grandpa's voice came to me, on his way indoors.

'Imogen, I'll take the children inside — I have to lie down for an hour . . . Yes, yes, of course I'm all right! Just tired, and can you wonder, being disturbed at all hours — last night it must have been two o'clock! . . . Yes, well, insomnia is one thing, you can get pills for that. You can tell young Tim from me, I shan't put up with much more of it!'

He went grumbling on his way, dragging a protesting Barney. For an instant more I sat still and silent. Only an instant.

I knew now why I hadn't given Damien a definite answer. My mind hadn't been able to face the truth — but now it could no longer be avoided. Quite simply, I couldn't walk out on the household until this horrific suspicion of mine had been settled, one way or the other.

I stood up deliberately. It had to be done now.

'Max!' I called out. I hurried across the grass to him.

'Hello there. I saw you were back — I didn't want to pester you right away. How's Damien?'

'Oh. In top form — full of Eastern promise! Max, have you heard that the prowler was on the loose again?'

'Last night. Yes, I know,' he said gravely. 'And Grandpa heard Tim come in. The old man doesn't seem to have associated the two, but — '

'You did. So did I!'

'It's still a very wild suspicion. But I heard this time there was a footprint, so I was intending to tell you all about it.'

'I'm going to ask Tim. I'll ask him now! I want you to be a witness.'

'Certainly,' he agreed more gravely still. 'I admire your courage. It won't be very easy — or pleasant.

'It's going to be horrible! It just has to be done, that's all.'

Between us, we planned our campaign. Max sought a highly curious Imogen to ask if she would 'stand in' for Tim for a few minutes. I looked into the kitchen to summon Tim in casual fashion and make some excuse to Monica.

I had chosen the dining room for this most difficult interview. It stood empty, the chairs lined up, a bowl of semi-wild single pink roses on the table. The laughter of Imogen's engagement party was long gone. Max stood awkwardly by the old marble fireplace.

'In here, please!' I told Tim tersely.

'Yes ma'am.' He complied with exaggerated meekness. 'What have I done?'

'Nothing, I hope. That's what we're here to find out. If we're way out of line, I'm sorry. We — we've some questions to ask you — '

'All right then, ask me!' he invited a little restively.

It was then that all pretence of normality fled. On an impulse I pounced on the door, shut and locked it and shoved the key into my pocket.

'Come on, Tim. I want the truth from you — and this time I'm going to get it. As you see, I've a witness here. We're all staying in here till you've told us all we want to know, do you understand?' I demanded.

'Give the girl an Oscar! Have you been seeing too many gangster movies, or what?' he said curtly. His face was becoming tense and angry.

'No, I haven't. Maybe you have! Look, I don't know how to say this — but we have to know for certain whether you're really some kind of sick-in-the-head marauder — or are you just trying to give a good imitation of one?' I paused there a moment groping for words.

'Supposing — just supposing — we called in the police to match up the footprint the prowler left last night when you were wandering around in the night heaven knows where! What would the answer be? Come on, can't you see I'm worried to death? What have you got to say!'

Whatever it was, he didn't say it, not one word. I could feel my heart racing and racing. His eyes had wavered from mine.

'There's always been something strange about you!' I forced out accusation on painful accusation. 'The way you arrived here, the way you've behaved — oh, Imogen spotted it too, so did Max! For all we know you were on the run when you first turned up and told Monica a hard luck story so you could hide away here! How do we even know you're Tim East at all, after what poor little Angel did?'

'You can keep Angel right out of it,' he muttered.

'She can't be kept out. Not when the poor child signed a form at the school fête Angelique West and was so very upset about it!'

'Oh, lord. Did she do that?' His face screwed up momentarily.

'She did! And there has to be an explanation. And we intend to find out what it is. If you're an ordinary, innocent citizen, OK, what have you got to fear? But if you're *not* . . . '

He had dropped his concealing tinted glasses on the table, and his dark eyes were looking straight into mine, this time holding my angry gaze no less angrily.

'All right. You've asked for it, you're not going to like it. Suppose it's all true, all you've been saying. What would Miss Great Detective Harrison do about it?'

'If it's true — I — I don't know what

I'd do about it . . . ' I stammered.

'Tim,' I breathed. 'Tim! Please, don't play games with me!'

I knew this was no game even before he answered me, 'I'm not playing games. And I'm not your 'ordinary, innocent citizen.' So does that satisfy you? Now will you give me that key? Please?'

'No, I won't. Not till you tell me the whole truth.'

I went on standing shakily, stubbornly, in front of the locked door. He took a step towards me, and then another. His face now was pale and furious — and most of all I saw in it the beginnings of a trapped panic that struck me like a blow.

It was then that Max intervened, quietly moving between us to forestall any attempt to grab that disputed door key.

'Simmer down, both of you. Let's not have too many histrionics here. Tim, I think we do need the whole story from you. Most of all, don't you think you owe it to Mrs Hale? She took you into her home as one of the family, she put all kinds of trust in you, she needn't have done that . . . '

Pulled up short, I was impressed by his authority. So long and so totally overshadowed by Damien, this commanding, unflurried Max had qualities I never even suspected.

'I know all she's done for Angel and me,' Tim said abruptly.

'Well then,' Max prompted. 'We're waiting.'

So we were. It seemed as though we had been shut in this room for hours already. The clock over the fireplace ticked ponderously. Outside were shouts of children, a flurry of far-off voices in the world beyond the window.

I saw Tim look round at that tempting window, plainly uncertain whether to submit to Max's questions or try making a break that way to freedom.

Probably the only reason he didn't try to escape was a sudden crescendo of the voices outside. There were screams, urgent shouts, people running.

And above it all, Greg's stentorian voice rose shrill with terror.

'Help! Help! Quick, somebody help! Angel fell down the big hole — miles and *miles* down the hole . . .'

It was Max, forgetful of prowlers and mysteries, who exclaimed in dawning horror, 'My God . . . not the well?'

We had, of course, two wells. The shallow dried-up one, with a picturesque but useless ancient pump beside it, was carefully enclosed in railings. The lengendary 'Deep Well' for which the old house had been named had never yet been discovered. Not until now.

★　★　★

Outside in the hot sunshine I was miraculously calm, holding tight to a now hopelessly sobbing Greg, ordering a ring of alarmed and curious café customers, 'Please keep well back, please don't get in the way!'

From somewhere out of sight came fitfully the faint and pitiful cries of Angel. Max and a grim-faced Tim and a couple of strong young motorbike lads already had ropes and flashlights on the scene, a tow-line from someone's car was being anchored around a massive treetrunk.

The distraught Greg had sobbed out what had happened. He had chased Angel with his toy gun, into the strictly forbidden rear part of the grounds which someone had left open — and among the tumbledown outbuildings, clambering over a pile of rubble, the little girl had plunged straight through a rotted wooden cover over the deep, dark, narrow well-shaft.

'She'll be dead — she'll be drowned!' Greg kept wailing.

'I've rung the fire brigade — and everybody else!' Imogen announced shakily. 'Shouldn't we wait till they get here?'

'No. She might struggle and slip further down,' I whispered. 'She must be stuck somehow, or else — we probably wouldn't hear her still crying . . . '

'Then let me go down on the rope! I'm slim, aren't I?'

'So is Tim. He's going down to her,' I said. 'He has to.'

Indeed, Angel's father was countenancing no offers from anyone. The attempted rescue was already going ahead.

One of the bikers, with a 'muscles' T-shirt, pony-tail and tattoos, seemed to know what he was doing. 'OK, mate,' he was telling Tim, 'got the light tied on tight? Me and Des'll see to this end. But watch yourself! — it's going to be tricky.'

'Let's get started! If I can't bring her up I'll just hang on to her . . . ' Tim said tersely.

I had one last glimpse of his face. There was no vestige of fear in it now.

'For goodness sake, he's ill, you know. He could be very ill! Does he have to go down there head-first?' I babbled to Imogen.

'I suppose he must,' she breathed, 'or else he — he might not have space to manoeuvre and tie the other rope to her, would he? Lorrie, I feel sick, I don't think I can watch . . . '

She did watch, nonetheless. Everyone stood there riveted to this sudden desperate drama in the leafy gardens.

The approaching sirens of a fire engine and an ambulance tore into the waiting stillness. A police car wasn't far behind. Imogen had done a very thorough job of summoning help.

Suddenly, there were invading uniforms and organised bustle. Still trembling in my arms, Greg watched them with dazed fascination. Heaven be praised, their journeys had all been wasted. The child was safe. Max and the two young bikers, hauling on their ropes, had brought Tim back to the surface — and not only was Angel tied in a loop of line, his hands were locked around her as though they would never let go.

Many willing pairs of hands received

the pair of them. Angel was dirty and dishevelled, but apart from minor scrapes and bruises, seemed completely unharmed.

Tim, equally grimy, with Angel clinging round his neck, shook hands with the triumphant pair of bikers, extended a hand also to Max — and then doubtfully drew it back again. People were slapping Tim on the back and congratulating him. There was a babble of voices now all the tension was over. I realised it was Max who was giving explanations to the various authorities. I was deeply grateful to have him there.

As well, an eager representative of the local press was in attendance — whether he had somehow got wind of the incident or merely called in for tea I never knew — who was taking pictures and scribbling notes.

After that, I wasn't sure what happened to Tim. Monica, whose wits so seldom deserted her, nudged me sharply in the ribs.

'Lorraine, fetch Imogen away from that camera and both of you get some more tea brewed, don't just stand there . . . and start on those trays of fruit cake. Come on, everything half-price and we'll still double the day's takings!'

'Monny, you're a hard-headed woman,' I accused. It wasn't true, of course. That flaming-bright head of hers might be well screwed on businesswise, but her heart was infinitely warm and caring. This plunge back into solid normality was her way of reacting to the ordeal we had just been through.

With trade buzzing in the café, I couldn't give it my attention for long. Tim was missing, and I slipped away to search for him. There was no telling what that rescue operation might have done to him. As for the scene it had interrupted the locked room. I could hardly believe that had ever happened.

Tim wasn't in Monica's downstairs room, where Angel lay on the bed with Grandpa and Monica in kind attendance — repeatedly asking, 'Where's my daddy? Will you fetch my daddy?'

'Will you, Lorraine?' Monica asked. 'We've rung Dr Basehart just to be on the safe side. But fretting for her dad is doing her no good at all!'

'I'll find him,' I said briefly.

Tim wasn't upstairs in his own domain. He wasn't anywhere around the café or kitchen. Unless he had stowed away in the departing fire-engine, it was a mystery. He certainly would have given a wide berth to the police car, whose driver was still talking to Max by the front door . . .

One idea my mind kept churning up, I simply would not believe. Tim wouldn't have run off into the blue leaving Angel behind. Whatever the truth I had almost uncovered, he would never do that . . .

There was still somewhere else to look, perhaps the most obvious place. I hurried round to the rear gardens, the gate now securely padlocked. Always this wild area had been a favourite of Tim's. Not waiting to fetch the key, I scrambled inelegantly over the gate. At first everything seemed deserted, the undergrowth trampled down by the recent influx of feet. Then I heard a human sound, like a gasp of anguish or effort. I called out, 'Tim, I'm coming! Where are you?'

I found him a moment later, by the well. A heavy old door, labelled in huge letters DANGER, had been dragged temporarily across to seal off that treacherous hole. A rope still hung from a closeby tree. It seemed to me that Tim was replacing the door in position over the well. He looked utterly exhausted, and yet in some strange way triumphant.

'Angel wants you! What are you doing out here?' I burst out.

'Just — making this thing safe.' He was scarcely able to speak.

'No, you're not. It *was* safe.' The position of the rope, and the way he was struggling for breath and shaking leaves from his hair, brought sudden enlightenment.

'Are you crazy, or are you stark, staring mad? You've been down that hole again, haven't you? Do you want to kill yourself outright and be done with it?'

He made a move towards an old bundle of something wrapped in mouldering plastic. He had failed to hide it from me, and now he was too exhausted to do more than claw it nearer, as he flopped on the ground to recover.

'What's that?' I demanded. 'You wouldn't risk life and limb to bring up some old rubbish from down there!' I made a grab for it, forcibly resisting his weak attempt to stop me. Whatever that bundle contained, it was quite heavy.

In another moment I knew why, as the wrappings tore away. On the rough grass fell a heap of jewellery, a stray sunbeam through the leaves glinting eerily on mellow gold, frosty diamonds, fiery rubies, a most beautiful deep-green emerald pendant. As well as that collection, there were twisted silver candlesticks, an antique figurine, a filigree casket, spilling out into the summer daylight from their gloomy incarceration. There was also money. Lots of it.

'So — so this is your horrible secret, is it? This wouldn't be — the proceeds of a robbery, by any chance?' It was all I could do to find words.

'All right. Now you know. I've been searching for this stuff all over! You wanted the truth, I said you wouldn't like it!'

'Yes, you did say that.' I dropped to my knees, carefully gathering together the scattered hoard. 'Then — this is why you wanted to stay at this house . . . and why you've been prowling around the neighbourhood at dead of night scaring decent folk out of their wits!' I gave a mirthless snort of laughter. 'You're a pretty inefficient burglar, aren't you, forgetting where you buried the loot?'

'Not really. I was only about half conscious when I hid the stuff. I'd just crashed the car, hadn't I?'

There was no way he could keep the rest of the story from me. A few more insistent questions brought the events of a fateful stormy night, many months ago, all too vividly to life.

He told me how he and his partner, Barry, were making a getaway from a Sussex county house — Barry master-minded the robbery — he knew about locks and alarm systems — and Tim assisted and drove the vehicle. There were high winds, violent thunder and rain. Cutting through Abbots Lane at speed, the car skidded out of control into a tree. Barry, not much hurt, grabbed most of the night's haul and fled — leaving a badly injured Tim.

But, although almost insensible, Tim crawled into the grounds of a neigh-bouring house, through a crumbled wall, to hide the bundle of 'loot' — his only light the eerie flicker of lightning, the wild trees heaving around him. He had just struggled back to the car, in the dazed hope of destroying any identification, when the wreckage burst into flames. He lost consciousness, and was found in the roadway. The fire and torrential rain removed all traces of his desperate trip to hide this part of the stolen fortune.

Recovering slowly from severe injuries, he realised there was a blank in his mind. He remembered the robbery, the getaway, even the shattering impact with the tree. He could not remember where the 'treasure' was hidden — only a vague impression of storm-drenched gardens, a looming old house revealed fitfully by the lightning. All else was pain and darkness.

So, when finally he could leave the hospital and rescue Angel from the mercies of Mrs Briggs, he returned to the district to seek temporary work, as a pretext for hanging around the neighbourhood. That was where Monica came in. He had intended staying a few days at most. He hadn't reckoned on becoming so deeply involved in The Lodge. He hadn't reckoned, most of all, with one of the derelict outbuildings having collapsed during the intervening months, so covering with rubble the site where 'his' share of the stolen hoard awaited retrieval.

'It's *not* yours! Not the tiniest part of it is yours!' I flared at him.

'Good grief, Tim, how could you? How could you? And how many others did you do, if I can believe one single word you tell me?'

'No others. This was the one and only.' He was sitting on a broken wall, pale-faced, as exhaustion faded a little his manner more defensive and sullen. 'I'll tell you why I did it. Because I saw what happened to my mother — she was pushed around until she died of overwork and underpay and every sort of cruel disappointment! I watched it happen. And I'm not watching it happen to Angel! She'll get her chances. She won't lose out for want of what it'll cost to get her started and successful and happy . . . '

The vision of the gifted, dark-eyed

child so lately in mortal danger, whose voice had just piteously begged me 'Fetch my daddy!' was too much. Tears of shock and grief flooded my eyes, and wouldn't be forced back. I knew what I ought to do. Every fibre of me shrank from doing it.

'But this isn't the way . . . Tim, she loves you so much, you're the whole world to her — more than the dancing will ever be! What do you think it'll do to her if — if you end up in prison?' I whispered.

'I see. You're going to turn me in, aren't you?' he said shortly.

How could I turn him in? How could I *not* turn him in?

I heard someone coming. With a deft movement Tim swept a heap of dead leaves over that glimmering pile on the ground between us. I looked round in dazed unreality at Max. I felt as though glaring guilt must be written huge and clear on my face.

'Hello,' he greeted us mildly. 'Why are you two hiding away here? — Angel is crying for you, Tim. Everyone has left except that local newshound, he won't budge without interviewing the Hero of the Hour, I warn you!'

The Hero of the Hour. Momentarily, I looked at Tim and he looked at me.

'Thanks,' I said quite stonily, 'we're coming now, Max. We were just making sure it's safe out here.'

The hours that followed that most extraordinary day were themselves far from ordinary.

Dr Basehart came and went, leaving a very mild sedative for Angel to take at bedtime. All evening, no-one seemed to stop talking, at least, barring Tim, who for once sat silently with Angel curled on his lap, and was fêted and waited upon. He looked embarrassed at all the admiring attention.

And well he might, I reflected.

The rescue was discussed over and over. Generous gifts would be posted on to the two helpful bikers. Max's presence of mind, Tim's bravery, were praised again and again. But also, there were other topics of excitement. The world hadn't stood still while I was away in London.

'My parents are coming to stay,' Imogen informed me, 'and Wayne'll be here a few days, too. Dad's a bit better just now, he'll have a car door to door, and he can use Monny's ground floor bedroom. Oh, I'm dying to see them and show them this place *and* my engagement ring!'

'How lovely for you all,' I approved. 'But if they use Monica's room — '

'No problem,' my cousin broke in decisively. 'I can get myself up and down the stairs. Maybe sideways like a crab, but I get there — don't I, Tim?'

'You do!' he agreed. 'Didn't I promise you would?'

'You did, Dr East!' She smiled at him across the room.

Indeed, this evening she was bustling around, albeit with a walking stick, once again in charge of her household — and wholly forgetful of being an invalid. I was delighted for her. I was delighted, too, for Imogen.

Meantime I had my own story to tell, of course, which amazingly had been pushed from centre stage since I arrived back. Now, I described Damien's exciting plans to visit the Orient. It was fortunate Max had just left to go back to the Riverside overnight. These would be, for him, the reverse of joyful tidings.

'That's what you really want, is it?' Monica said.

'Of course she does!' Imogen flourished a dishmop in my support. 'It sounds fabulous! We'll miss you a lot, Lorrie, but you certainly deserve a good time after all the work and effort you've put in here for us!'

I was suprised and touched by that unexpected tribute from the careless and casual Imogen. Equally so by old Mr Hale's gruff agreement, 'Yes, you've done an excellent job here, young lady. Though why you want to hike off to these outlandish places I don't know, the food will ruin your insides for a start!'

Monica said very little, but what she did say meant most of all. 'But for you, this place would still be an unsuccessful dump. It would have shut down anyway when I had my accident. It's taken me a while to appreciate everything you've done here . . . now I can only say, nothing's too good for you.'

Quite suddenly I could say nothing at all. I fled in choked confusion.

My feet drew me irresistibly to the top of the house. The stairs and landings were dimly lighted. The door of Tim's room was ajar, and I peered round. Upon her bed by the far wall, Angel lay in a deep sleep. Like a statue beside her, her father sat gazing down at her, his face stern and preoccupied.

'Tim!' I whispered, and he put a finger to his lips. When he joined me on the landing, I still spoke very softly. 'Tell me, please. What have you done with — with the you-know-what? It's not still out there?'

'What do you think? Credit your friendly neighbourhood burglar with a little sense. No, it's not out there, it's in a safe place.

'Yes, I thought it might be. Tim, listen to me. Swear to me solemnly you won't run off without telling me first! Swear to me!'

'What are you going to do?'

'I don't know! Can't you see it's driving me crazy *not* knowing? But till I decide, you've got to swear to me!' I hissed fiercely.

'All right. Angel's not fit to travel anyway.' He lifted his right hand in the manner of a courtroom oath. 'I swear. Satisfied?'

I nodded and turned on my heel.

Presently, the household drifted off to bed, far later than usual. For hours I lay staring at the darkness struggling to decide what to do.

It was just getting light, a summer dawn abundant with birdsong, when finally I must have drifted into sleep.

It was broad daylight. Imogen was standing by my bed with a cup of tea.

'What's the time? What are you

doing? Where's Tim?' I stammered hazily.

'Tim's fine. We're all fine! We let you sleep on — but it's high time to wakey-wakey, nearly ten o'clock! Are you all right? You will be in a minute!'

'Why — why will I?' I rubbed heavy eyes.

'Because downstairs there's a gorgeous, tall, dark and handsome, blue-eyed man, sipping our best coffee from one of our best cups and waiting for you.'

'Max?' I said painfully.

She shook her head and laughed, and waltzed out of the room.

7

'How are you, Lorraine? I'm so sorry you all had such a bad time here yesterday. I came straight down as soon as I heard.'

It was Damien's high-browed, aquiline face that lifted to greet me. They were Damien's blue eyes. It was hard to believe in yesterday. It was hard to believe Damien was really here and not a wistful dream . . .

'It's you! But — how on earth did you know about — ?'

'Max rang me.'

Max. I should know by now never to discount his unobtrusive thoughtfulness.

'I was telling your cousin here — ' Damien glanced round at Monica, who stood by gravely and sharply watchful. 'It sounds as though the poor child had quite an escape. I think you're all to be congratulated for your presence of mind.'

'Most of us did nothing at all,' Monica said. 'We stood around and chewed our nails. Max was as steady as a rock. The child's father took all the risks.'

'Nevertheless. It would have been easy to panic and make matters worse. You've already had more than your fair share of troubles here — oh, yes, I know all about them. I'm so glad to see you on your feet again and looking so well . . . '

That most devastating of smiles clearly got through even to Monica. It wasn't just charm that Damien had, it was something far more telling. He knew how to use it, of course, when he wanted something. I discovered very quickly what it was he wanted now.

'So I can assume Lorraine's invaluable services are no longer essential to you here, Mrs Hale? You seem to have everything running very smoothly!'

Monica cleared her throat gruffly.

'That's entirely due to her management skills. But — yes, of course, she's entirely a free agent. Now if you'll excuse me, there's work to do, I can't stand around gossiping.'

She stomped off out of the room in her ungainly but increasingly brisk manner. I stood there feeling more unusually shy, aware of my face burning, my heart drumming.

'So,' Damien said. 'You're free as air, you heard it from the lady's own lips. I think that was the main stumbling-block in the way of my Eastern journey?'

'One of them,' I muttered.

'Perhaps I can remove the rest. Will you come over here a moment?'

I approached, doubtfully, wonder-ingly. I sat down on the chair beside his mainly because my legs had turned to rubber.

'I'm sure this is totally unfair, I should wait for a calmer moment — but I want you to understand something. Yesterday I didn't make it quite clear, did I? I told you I'd missed you very much ... but it's not just because you're the best secretary I've ever had or am likely to have ... it's you yourself I missed, don't you realise that? Just being with you, just having you always beside me ... '

His hands had found both of my own. He leaned towards me.

'Now do you understand? It took that stupid fight we had a while ago to make me realise how much I care for you. I couldn't bear to lose you. I want to be with you for always. Do you believe me, Lorraine? Will you marry me?

'But — if you really love me — ' I blurted out.

'I do love you. Very much.'

'Then how about Cecilia Brand?' I demanded shakily. 'I thought — '

'Yes, I know what you thought. That was a mistake. Very unfortunate.'

'Unfortunate? Do you know what it did to me?' I quavered.

'I'm sorry. Cecilia is a lovely person,

but it was a mistake — I'm sure a mutual mistake. Haven't you heard she's going around with that young Swiss conductor?'

'Is she?' I whispered. You didn't hear things like that at The Lodge.

'His touch with Wagner was a little pedestrian when I last heard it. His touch with Cecilia seems more lively. He's taking her home to Zurich next month.'

'Are you sure? Are you quite sure? Have you spoken to her? Damien, I have to know before — '

'I'll ring her today and straighten it out. Does that satisfy you?'

'And — you'd really rather be married to the under-skivvy at The Lodge than that really beautiful, blonde girl and her wonderful violin playing?'

I got no further than that. His lips found mine, and there was no more thought or reason. Still unbelieving, I was in his arms, drawn close to him, enveloped in his nearness. The world had stopped revolving.

'No more Lodges and skivvyings for you, my dearest,' he whispered the words, his lips against my hair. 'From now on, only the best. When would you like the wedding? We could rush it before we go to Japan — or wait till afterwards and follow it up with a honeymoon in Barbados? Or maybe Capri?'

I didn't know, I couldn't think, I couldn't feel. Only I was conscious of his arms around me, this man I had idolised, I once thought I almost hated, I had lost and found. At last, I had truly found him! The dream-future he was sketching would be real and true. Fantasies and desolation were all behind me. The age of miracles wasn't past.

I wasn't quite sure what happened after that. We weren't alone any more, and Damien must have made a public announcement because people were congratulating us, Imogen giving me a gleeful hug, Grandpa gruffly shaking my hand, Max saying very, very quietly,

'I wish you both every happiness. From the bottom of my heart.'

Tim put his head round the door just once — and murmured to me, 'Well done!' whatever he meant by that. The children were playing noisily and no-one checked them.

'Can you stay here with us for a few days?' Monica was asking Damien. 'We've plenty of room. Home cooking, peace and quiet. Well, usually peace and quiet!' She added, as he raised one dark, expressive brow.

'I'd really like that. Sorry, it just can't be done at present. I've a meeting tomorrow in London — then it looks like I'll have to fly back to the States for a couple of days to tie up loose ends . . . Then there'll be the preparations for Japan — also a week-end in Derby with my mother. A packed schedule, that's why I'm hoping Lorraine will come back to London with me right away and help me through all of it. Will you?' he appealed to me.

I looked round at Monica.

'Go ahead! Just go!' she said.

'Are you quite sure?'

'Of course. I've plenty of help here — I wouldn't stand in your way for the world. The States, Japan, Bermuda — just go, with my blessing!'

I was horribly afraid I would break down and disgrace myself. Damien wouldn't care for any maudlin exhibitions.

He had planned lunch with someone at Brighton, it seemed. He would call back this afternoon for me, which would allow time to pack my things and say my farewells. Still in a dream I watched him drive off, the sun glinting on his car, one slender hand extended through the window in a parting flourish. I waved back. In a moment, I would wake up.

It was time to start packing. But there was one thing I must do first.

Luckily, Tim was alone in the kitchen, busy slicing up salad.

'It's all right, no more lurid scenes, Tim, just some straight talking. First of all — I want to thank you for not disappearing overnight.'

'I gave you my word I'd stay put, didn't I?'

'I know. It must have been difficult. Then I also want to thank you for all the help you've given Monica, we couldn't have got by without you — '

'Yes. Well.' He waved a tuft of lettuce impatiently. 'Just tell me what you're going to do. Are you going to the police or aren't you?'

'No.' I took a long breath. 'I know I should. But I've been thinking and thinking . . . especially about poor little Angel. Look, I'm sure there's much more good than bad in you!' It sounded a horribly smug and superior homily, but I couldn't prevent that. 'I want you to do one thing for me, I'm trusting you to do it! Find a way to return the stolen things anonymously to where they belong, or to the police, I don't care which. You can do that! And then take Angel and go and make a fresh start somewhere, try to do something with your life! Of course, the file on the robbery — and the prowlings — won't be closed, but if you're clever you might still get away with it all . . . '

'I see.' He laughed mirthlessly. 'Just like that. Dead easy.'

'I didn't say it was easy. I said that's what you have to do!'

'And that will clear your mind ready for the joys of Bermuda, will it?'

'No. Not completely, it won't. But — we've been through so much together, and I can't bear Angel to be hurt any more, and — ' My voice faltered and failed. The strength of character I was supposed to possess had all gone from me. 'I know it's a poor sort of compromise, but it's the best I can do. So — do you agree, or don't you?'

'Do I really have a choice?' he asked bitterly.

'Don't make me do something I'd hate to do. Please don't make me,' I said.

'You know if you keep your mouth

shut you'll be an accessory after the fact or whatever? Your Mr Blooming High-and-Mighty Clyde wouldn't take kindly to that, would he? Watch out he doesn't ditch you like yesterday's cold porridge!'

'How dare you insult Damien?' I flared at him. 'How dare you? He's worth a million of you, and you know it!'

'I daresay. Even now I'm in the money I couldn't fly off on cosy trips around the world. How many yachts and Rollers and gold nuggets did he offer to get you to go with him? Or was it just the whiter-than-white smile? I've seen crocodiles with fewer highly polished gnashers, I'm telling you!'

I was within an inch of striking him full in his insolent face. The furious retort that sprang to my lips was barely choked back as Imogen arrived and chirped brightly, 'Two more teas! — and are the ham salad sandwiches ready yet?'

'Coming up!' he told her. 'Pardon

me, Miss H. The workers have work to do.'

'Of course. Just answer me. Yes or no?' I muttered stiffly.

He buttered slices of bread quite viciosly. 'I'll think about it, all right?'

I went upstairs to start packing.

★   ★   ★

'I'll ring. I'll write. And of course, I'll see you before we go to Japan — I'll absolutely insist we come down and stay a couple of days,' I promised.

Damien's car was pulled up outside. He was loading in my much travelled luggage, off on the move again.

'Yes, send us some nice postcards, tantalise us!' Imogen said enviously. 'Have fun, don't work too hard — as if you would!'

Of Tim there was no sign, but Angel stood and looked at me in deep, deep, silent reproach. I couldn't quite trust myself to speak to her, but smiled and waved. Please heaven, I had saved her from more unhappiness. Please heaven, too, I wasn't breaking Max's heart as Damien almost broke mine a while ago. I glimpsed him standing next to Monica, lifting a hand in farewell.

There was no point in prolonging this parting. I waved once more at the group in the doorway, as Damien turned the car down the drive.

'I trust you had nothing to do with those.' He lifted a pained eyebrow as we passed the pot-bellied stone birds on the gateposts.

'They were here when we came. I've got quite attached to them!'

'You amaze me.' The eyebrow lifted higher.

Out on the open road, this long glorious Summer still reigned supreme. The trees stirred gently against an azure sky dappled with high cloud. There were wild flowers by the roadside, yellow and mauve and white. The slopes of Tall Hill rose in the sun, a few hikers toiling up its winding paths.

Deep Well Lodge was a closed chapter.

'I thought we could take in the Janinski piano recital tonight,' Damien was saying briskly. 'All of his usual crowd-pulling Chopin, but I promised him I'd look in. We should just about make it to the Albert Hall on time.'

'Yes. Good,' I agreed a little absently.

'That reminds me — the name you mentioned, 'Marie-Angelique.' I made a couple of calls and tracked the woman down for you. Not that there was much to find. Very mediocre, all tinsel and no talent. A few stage appearances, back-row flower girl or second understudy, that kind of thing . . .'

'Oh. Is that all? But — I know she *could* have done a lot more, she had private troubles and just never had the chance to achieve higher things!'

'Maybe. The story of a lot of lives. These people have to make their minds up, don't they? If they don't give a hundred percent, what do they expect?'

Perhaps it was true. That made it no less sad.

I went on sitting there, and the music

still flowed over me, the surroundings still flashed past. When we reached a fair-sized town, traffic lights and congestion bogged us down, causing Damien's fingers to drum impatiently.

I stared at cars and shops and people through a great blur of ever increasing anguish. The pain of it grew and grew. It was no longer the sombre grandeur of Beethoven, or the emotion of the recent parting, that were building it up so uncontrollably within me.

What was I really doing in this car? Where was I really going? Where was I letting myself be taken by this cold, cold stranger sitting beside me?

'Damien — ' I whispered. He didn't hear me. My voice was lost in the music.

'Damien!' I tried again. This time I spotted a British Rail sign, I burst in upon swelling melody. 'Quick, turn left here! Then stop the car, please stop the car!'

The urgency of my voice made him juggle with the wheel and indicators to obey. He pulled up outside the railway station.

'What in heaven's name is the matter with you? I nearly hit that Volvo, didn't you see? This isn't the road we want!'

'I want it! I'm getting out of here. I — I have to go back.' I fumbled with the door, suddenly spilling out words. 'Damien, I'm sorry, but — I have to go back. I'll get a train to Abbeybridge — never mind my luggage, you can send it on, or keep it, or give it away, I don't care!'

'What are you saying?' He had switched off the music. His face was stern, his eyes firing with blue anger. 'Are you trying to tell me — ?'

'I can't go abroad with you and work with you, and — and I can't marry you. I'm sorry! I made a mistake . . . an unfortunate mistake . . . ' Unconsciously I quoted his own earlier words. Those cruel airy words. 'You can get another Marsha or Libby, just go to a good agency. You can go and find Cecilia, and good luck to her if you do.

You can do all sorts of things — but I can't be part of it, not any of it. I just want to go back. I have to go back!'

Already I had the door open and was scrambling out.

Then suddenly I was standing alone on the pavement, the car door banged shut. The vehicle roared away up the street. It was like a waking nightmare. I was shaking all over.

I stumbled into the station. As luck would have it, an Abbeybridge train was almost due.

For all I knew the journey could have been on the moon — or through legendary Japanese landscapes that I wouldn't see now. Abbeybridge Station came into view at last. I thought of ringing The Lodge. I thought of a taxi — but a bus outside was just swallowing a warm and weary queue and I raced to join it.

From the nearest bus stop to Abbots Lane I started running like a wild thing. The last few yards seemed to stretch to interminable miles. The vultures on the gateposts eyed me stonily.

The café must have shut early, and there was actually no work going on. The children were picnicking on the lawn, with cakes and drinks spread on a cloth. Amiably overseeing them, Monica and Max were sitting together at one of the white tables . . . sitting close together. His dark head was bent near her bright hair that had lighted to living flame in the sunshine.

Unless my eyes deceived me — and even at this distraught moment I knew they didn't — the two of them were holding hands like teenagers.

Max and Monica! Monica and Max, *not* Monica and Tim. Well, why not? Why not? Perhaps I had been incredibly blind or stupid or both — but it was better this way, very much better! At present I simply didn't care, not about that, nor the shocked consternation and amazement in all the faces that turned to me.

'Where's Tim? Is Tim still here?' I blurted out. Was I already too late?

Monica, pink faced, was stuttering unintelligibly, whether with shock or embarrassment. It was Max who answered.

'Tim went out to get a bus to the town. He seemed rather upset, he asked us to keep an eye on Angel for a while . . . Lorraine, what's the matter, why in the world are you back here? Did Damien — ?'

'Damien's gone to London, I got a train back — oh, I'll explain all that later! Can I borrow someone's car, any car? I have to find Tim, it's very, very urgent!'

Max's quiet unflappable voice had never seemed slower. 'Sorry. I'm charging the battery on mine. Monny's has a flat. If you can wait for half an hour — '

'Good grief,' I breathed. 'Max, I mean *now*! Never mind, I can run!'

I turned to Imogen as she appeared from the house, staring at me aghast as though I were the Ghost of Christmas Yet to Come. 'Imogen lend me your sandals! Hurry!'

I almost tore them from her feet, leaving her sitting on the step with her mouth hanging open.

There was just one more thing I had to find out, already halfway down the drive. 'Did Tim take anything with him? A bag — a parcel?'

'I think — yes, some sort of parcel,' Max supplied.

It was all I wanted to know. I started running, with sudden new strength born of stark urgency.

Tim was bound for the same bus route by which I had just arrived, but our paths hadn't crossed — so logically, either I was altogether too late and had missed him, or else he was taking the path through Holts Wood leading to the main road. I panted through the woodland like a fox before the hounds, ripping my skirt on a bramble, wading through nettles without feeling a pang. Where the path came out to the road, the bus halt was nearby, quite close to the Stables. There were none of Mrs Dawson-Blake's pupils waiting there now. There was just one fair-haired man, holding a weighty carrier bag.

'Thank goodness,' I breathed in all heartfelt reverence.

My arrival like a bolt from the blue had an even more shattering effect on him than on anyone. Ignoring his reaction completely I gasped out, 'Tim, what are you doing? Where do you think you're going with that?'

'Where do you think? To my own private Fagan to cash it all in.'

I gazed at him mutely, half believing.

'A chance would be a fine thing. You do a better job than the SAS, you do.' His voice was hard and bitter. 'You came back to make sure I followed orders, did you? If you want to know, I'm going one better. I'm taking this lot to the police, to finish the whole thing. Which means I'm walking straight into a prison sentence and you'll be able to soak up your Bermuda honeymoon sun in righteous peace.'

'I'm not going anywhere near Bermuda! I've called it all off! Shall I tell you why? Damien is a wonderful man, he — he's like an answer to a maiden's prayer, he's rich and handsome and witty and clever . . . but when you get close enough to him you find he hasn't got a heart, Tim. And you have more than anyone I know — so did you really think I could go swanning off across the world with him and leave you to face all this by yourself?'

I had collapsed back against the rough and spiky hedge, exhausted and tearful — and I clung to him, holding him close to me, in my joy and my sorrow in that deep, abiding, hidden love now in the open at last.

There was a green verge a little back from the road. I huddled on the grass in a heap, still clinging to Tim, careless of an occasional motorist passing us by. The bus didn't come. While it was delayed, I learned a great deal.

There by the roadside I poured out question after insistent question — and at long last I was getting my answers. He was too utterly shocked to resist.

It was a strange, sad narrative that came to me, partly jumbled, partly vividly clear. First and foremost, the 'Tim East' I had known all these weeks was in reality Emile Timothy West. Poor Angel had almost given the game away when once she signed her real name. She had been told the change would prevent Old Mother Briggs ever getting hold of her again — which more than explained her horror over her slip at the school fête.

I already knew how the young boy Emile had been left solitary when his young mother died and his English father had long ago deserted them.

I knew, too, about that unfulfilled longing of Tim's to become a vet. Now, I learned more. It had started with a stray, sick puppy which he and his mother once nursed until it died. After some wild youthful years, Tim actually struggled through to gain a place at a veterinary school. But at an early stage his studies were ended by serious illness — relating to a blow on the head he had received years before.

Though he recovered from the brain inflammation, his powers of concentration were gone, he was plagued by crippling headaches. He never returned to the veterinary school. Subsequently, he married a young nurse, Judy, who had looked after him. He did a few 'odd jobs', becoming bitter at being kept by his wife's long hours nursing. Meantime, Angel was born to them.

'I saw Judy's picture,' I whispered. 'She was lovely, Tim. Please tell me the rest . . . '

He told me, staring down the road with screwed-up dark eyes. Tragedy had followed tragedy, during a frugal caravan holiday, a prey to headaches and changeful moods, he slammed out one day after a fierce quarrel leaving Judy much upset — and, probably due to her preoccupied carelessness after that scene, the caravan caught fire. A rescuer saved the child's life, but Judy died.

Angel's rescuer was one Barry Tate, a mate of Tim's at one of the Homes with whom he once absconded to 'live rough' for several days and nights on the London streets. Barry, the one person with whom he had kept in contact, later carved out a career for himself in petty crime, some not so petty. Using his rescue of Angel as some sort of lever he demanded help with a 'job' for a share of the takings. Tim, simply not caring any more, was tempted by the thought of securing Angel's future, the only thing that still mattered to him in the world.

What remained, I already knew, or could guess. On a wild October night the robbery took place at the country home of a wealthy financier, and just past Abbey Bridge the getaway car skidded out of control. Barry callously made off with the major part of the haul — bound, Tim believed, for foreign shores.

Tim, hazily determined not to be a loser yet again, managed to hide the rest of the loot. When eventually he left hospital, he collected Angel from her foster home, with a changed identity to avoid any link with the still remembered car smash, he arrived on Monica's doorstep in search of temporary work. Once the hidden bundle was found he could quietly disappear . . . and whatever happened to him, Angel should have her ballet school and achieve her future destiny!

'She has Judy's smile . . . sometimes I can't bear to see it, you know? And other times . . . I remember my mother dancing for me when I was a kid, in a garden somewhere, with handfuls of flowers and a white rose in her hair . . . '

A back-row flower girl with more tinsel than talent. Damien's cruel, chill words would be locked for always in my heart. I saw the tears on Tim's face. Impulsively, I rocked him in my arms like a child.

'It'll be all right. It will. Angel will have her future, we'll see to it — but we need to see about you first, don't we? Tim, you made bad mistakes — but most of us make mistakes, look at the way I've thrown away precious time chasing after something I didn't really want!' I declared with impassioned force. 'And now I'm *not* going to sit back and see your life ruined over this, do you hear me? I'll get you a good lawyer, we'll do the best we can — if the worst comes to the worst I'll wait for you, I'll stand by you every inch of the way — but please heaven it won't come to that — '

I paused for breath, and he didn't attempt to answer me. I wasn't finished yet.

'Most important of all, we're going to get you well! I know people with contacts, there's got to be a specialist somewhere who can help you — if he's living and breathing I'll find him! Tim, it's going to be a tough time for us, but we'll get through it somehow. You're a survivor, if ever there was one, you and Angel both . . . '

For once his facility of quick-fire response, the bright, sharp, streetwise assurance learned in a hard school, had completely deserted him. He seemed almost bowled over by that shower of words. Still I ploughed on, but now more softly and hesitantly.

'I'll be a true mother to Angel for always, I promise. I — I'm not awfully good with children, but Angel is different! She's always been very, very special to me. I wouldn't try to take Judy's place, but . . . '

Perhaps I was taking too much for granted. I started to pull away from him, but he held on to me. I realised he had lifted his head, there was even just a glimmer of the old mischief breaking through.

'This is so sudden, Miss H. Are you trying to tell me something?'

'Yes. I'm trying to say — I love you. Now I've said it, go on and laugh if you want to! Tim, I'd marry you tomorrow if you wanted me, silver candlesticks and all! But — probably you don't want me . . . '

'What gave you that idea?' he broke in quickly. 'I want you a whole lot more than those rotten candlesticks. Ever since the first day I came here, and then more and more. I never thought there'd be anyone else after Judy, but I couldn't help the way I felt about you. I reckoned I wouldn't stand a snowball's chance while you had Max and Damien to choose from — '

'Max is a wonderful friend. But just a friend.'

'And Damien?' he insisted. 'I thought you were besotted with the guy.'

'So did I,' I whispered. 'I found out today. I think it started when you were so angry with me for going off with him — you were, weren't you? Angry and terribly hurt — '

'Yes, it hurt. I could have throttled him. And you!'

'I know. I realised that afterwards — I

guessed then that maybe you cared for me just a little. And when Damien was driving me off, suddenly it all went wrong, the things he was saying to me. That's when I really found out about him. Tim, I just suddenly knew I couldn't go through with it, I — I just had to get out of that car and get back to you!'

'It must have taken some courage to stand him up like that,' he said. 'But — maybe you should have stayed put, no matter what. You and me — it wouldn't really work out, would it? There's your family for a start.'

'If they don't accept you, then they can do without me, too! No, I'm sure it will be all right. We'll go out to Norway to see my father as soon as we can, it'll be a wonderful treat for Angel. And the others — I know them very well now. Imogen will think it's a thrilling chunk out of a soap opera — Grandpa has a very kind heart behind that bristling exterior — and Monica — ' I paused a moment. 'Monica has a lot of time for you. You'll get the sharp end of her tongue, you'll also get all the help she can give. You've done so much for her. I really do believe it was your support and understanding that dragged her through a very dark tunnel . . . '

'I'm not going to drag you down to my level.'

'What nonsense! We'll both go up and up together! You'll see,' I said eagerly.

The bus was trundling up. Eyes peered at us from a passing car. I cared for none of them. Gazing into the face close to mine, the fair, freckled, trouble-scarred face that meant everything to me, I felt his lips warm and strong upon mine. I gave up my mouth to his kiss. I surrendered my heart and my soul to the reality of a love discovered almost too late.

The next motorist cruised to a standstill. I recognised Max's car, which he must have managed to start somehow. Next to him was Monica, holding Barney, she passed the child over to him and climbed out.

'Lorraine — Tim — what do you two think you're doing? We were so worried, we had to follow on and look for you! Will you tell me what's going on?'

'It'll take some telling.' I scrambled up, dusting off grass and leaves. 'Oh, I'm so glad you came! Bless you, Monny. If we could scrounge a lift into town — '

'Of course. Anything we can do to help!'

'Bless you,' I repeated. And then I had to ask, in a piercing whisper, 'Am I dreaming all this, or are you and Max?'

'Maybe we are,' she said gruffly. 'It's early days yet. If you really want to know, I realise your love-life is a complete monkey-puzzle, but you were a fool to bypass him! He's a very nice person, and the main reason he followed you around — which got on your nerves so much — was because he thought you were being hurt by his brother, he felt a family responsibility to protect you. That's how nice a person you shut the door on!'

'But I'd like him as a cousin-in-law,' I hinted. 'I really would.'

'You're taking a lot for granted, miss!' she retorted, but I believed, with joy and gratitude, that Maxwell Clyde would presently be part of the family. I was quite sure of it.

'So after all the fireworks it's going to be off with Damien and on with Tim?' Monica was saying. 'I despair of keeping up with you. Are you sure you know what you're doing?'

'I thought I wanted Damien more than anything in the world. I was so wrong. I promise you, now I've never been more sure of anything in my life . . . '

I tugged Tim forward. Understand-ably, he was hanging back.

There would be time later for all this chit-chat. At present we needed to get into the town while our courage lasted. Max, reaching over to open the rear door, asked mildly, 'Where to?'

'I'll tell you as we go along. We have

— rather an awkward errand. Oh dear, you're going to have quite a shock, I'm not sure how to tell you — '

'Don't waffle, just try us!' Monica invited, so completely her old self again.

I was thinking, as she settled herself again beside Max and Barney was passed once more between them, that if indeed a whole new future was dawning for her and for her children, no-one deserved it more than she did.

For one passing instant, the speaking likeness in Max's face brought me a vision of Damien. I had no regrets. I would never regret.

Angel was curled up in the back of the car, her eyes wide and anxious, and she launched herself at Tim and climbed instantly into his lap. I sat very close to them. I stroked the child's blonde hair.

'Don't be frightened, Angel,' I whispered to her. 'Whatever happens, darling, don't ever be frightened again . . . '

There might be heartbreak for all of us at the end of this road, but it had to be met — and it would pass, as all else passed. I knew I would somehow find strength to see it through, in the depth of my love for the man and the child who meant so much more to me than the brittle lustre of Damien's worldl

For this at last was the prize of gold waiting for me! This blending of transient pain and lasting glory. When the pain was ended, when this unforgettable rainbow summer was long over, still the enduring glory of love would be mine for always.

For always.

We do hope that you have enjoyed reading this large print book.

Did you know that all of our titles are available for purchase?

We publish a wide range of high quality large print books including:
Romances, Mysteries, Classics
General Fiction
Non Fiction and Westerns

Special interest titles available in large print are:
The Little Oxford Dictionary
Music Book, Song Book
Hymn Book, Service Book

Also available from us courtesy of Oxford University Press:
Young Readers' Dictionary
(large print edition)
Young Readers' Thesaurus
(large print edition)

For further information or a free brochure, please contact us at:
Ulverscroft Large Print Books Ltd.,
The Green, Bradgate Road, Anstey,
Leicester, LE7 7FU, England.
Tel: (00 44) **0116 236 4325**
Fax: (00 44) **0116 234 0205**

THE DOCTOR WAS A DOLL

Claire Vernon

Jackie runs a riding-school and, living happily with her father, feels no desire to get married. When Dr. Simon Hanson comes to the town, Jackie's friends try to match-make, but he, like Jackie, wishes to remain single and they become good friends. When Jackie's father decides to remarry, she feels she is left all alone, not knowing the happiness that is waiting around the corner.

TO BE WITH YOU

Audrey Weigh

Heather, the proud owner of a small bus line, loves the countryside in her corner of Tasmania. Her life begins to change when two new men move into the area. Colin's charm overcomes her first resistance, while Grant also proves a warmer person than expected. But Colin is jealous when Grant gains special attention. The final test comes with the prospect of living in Hobart. Could Heather bear to leave her home and her business to be with the man she loves?

RUNAWAY HEART

Shirley Allen

Manuella's grandfather intends to marry her to the odious Don Miguel, and persuades her father to agree to the match. In desperation, Manuella, who is half-gypsy, runs away to her other family. When the gypsy camp is attacked by Don Miguel, her father and their followers, she is rescued by two Englishmen, Jonathan Wilde and Roderick Maine. Manuella falls in love with Roderick — but will he consider her suitable to be his wife?

ZABILLET OF THE SNOW

Catherine Darby

For Zabillet, a young peasant girl growing up in the tiny French village of Fromage in the mid-fourteenth century, a respectable marriage is the height of her parents' ambitions for her. But life is changing. Zabillet's love for a handsome shepherd is tested when she is invited to join the La Neige household, where her mistress, Lady Petronella, has plans for her grandson, Benet. And over all broods the horror of the Great Death that claims all whom it touches.